PURGATORY CITY

THROUGH THE GATES BOOK ONE

REBECCA ROYCE

SKYE MACKINNON

Peryton Press

[1]

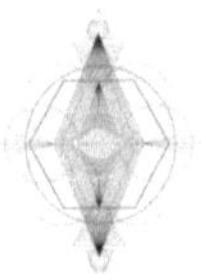

The gates loomed in front of me like hungry jaws waiting to swallow me whole. This was the moment they'd decide whether I lived or died. There was no other option. No returning to the Blastlands, no chance of ever seeing my friends again. These gates only went one way. Maybe they spit out the bones of the dead at some point, but they didn't let anyone leave alive.

Was I ready to die? I nodded. Yes, I was. There was no future for me in the Blastlands, no way of surviving for much longer. Everyone was starving and killing each other. Going through the gates might actually be a quicker, better way to die than staying out here.

Slowly, the queue moved forward, and with it, the stench of sweat and sickness drifted across the air. It was particularly hot today, absolutely scorching. No wonder people around me were smelly. I was, too, but I didn't want to examine that further. I already felt less than human, and knowing how much I stank would just increase that feeling.

One by one, the people in front of me walked through the gates, each of them swallowed by the darkness beyond.

Nobody knew exactly what the city on the other side of the Wall looked like. All we had were rumors of beauty, wealth, and as much good as you can eat. Even if the stories were exaggerated, there had to be a nugget of truth behind the myth.

A man behind me stumbled, and I turned to help him up, but two guards were faster, pulling him out of the queue. They dragged him to a small building next to the gates and pushed him inside. I wasn't sure if I wanted to know what was going to happen to him. We were coming here to work. That was going to be our purpose in Purgatory City. If we weren't strong enough to work, then we weren't of any use for the people ruling this place.

Finally, the woman in front of me stepped into the darkness. It was my turn. Now that I was standing in front of the gates, it was clear that it wasn't actual darkness, just shadows hiding whatever lay beyond. That was a little more reassuring.

The guards held me back, their white uniforms a stark contrast to all the dust-covered people around them. They wore gloves that by now were full of dirt from touching us. I wondered what they had to think of us. People living outside the City, unclean, uneducated, wild. Sickness was rife in the Blastlands and many of us died long before we reached old age.

"Go now." One of the guards grunted and pointed toward the gates. I took a deep breath and started to walk into the shadows. It was time for my new life to begin and hopefully not end.

I braced for death to come for me right there. I didn't know what it would be like, since no one who died ever returned to tell us about the experience. Nothing happened.

"Step forward."

The instructions came from a voice farther along, where I couldn't see, somewhere in the shadows. That had to be a good sign. Didn't it? Rumors always said if death came, it came instantly, but maybe they were wrong, maybe it came later.

"Eileen Paine." The voice repeated my name a second before what light there was around me went black and the gate banged shut. I jumped, my hand coming reflexively up to my throat. "Age twenty. Parents: John and Lauren Paine. Both deceased. You are seeking refuge in Purgatory City. Say confirm if you confirm all of this to be true."

I hadn't given anyone this information about me, but it didn't surprise me that whoever it was making these decisions today knew everything about us.

"You are strong. Healthy. You are of above-average intelligence and hold no specific genetic markers that will make you get sick in the future."

Well... I supposed that was all good. "Um... thanks. Yes, I think I am those things. Confirmed or whatever."

"Approved. Step forward."

Darkness surrounded me. Where exactly did they want me to walk? I couldn't screw this up now. Not with my above-average intelligence. I steeled my spine. If they were trying to kill me, they'd have done so by now, and more easily than giving me impossible instructions to follow. I stepped forward. There was ground beneath my feet. That was good news. I kept walking. A light appeared ahead.

I forced myself to keep going, to stride toward that light. Light meant hope, light meant a future, light meant...

Cage doors shut around me, forming a perfect cube encasing my body. I grabbed onto the bars. What was happening? This wasn't what was supposed to be happening.

"Relax, Eileen Paine. When you wake up, you will be in what your people call Purgatory City. Welcome to the Game."

To the what?

A cool liquid coated my body. Where had that come from? I backed up, hitting the bars on the other side of the cage. I didn't understand. None of this made sense. All I wanted was a chance, a future. Not...

Whatever I would have thought vanished as blackness overtook me, taking me down, pulling me into sleep, whether I wanted to go or not.

With only distant awareness of what was happening to me, I collapsed in my cage, the bars on the bottom stopping my full descent but allowing my legs to dangle through toward a bottomless cavern. Or maybe I imagined that. In the place between wakefulness and sleep, I struggled and failed to remain conscious.

◆

I DREAMED.

I was back with my parents, before the bombs had taken out our home. My mother was young, beautiful, not beat up as she would be later. She reached out, caressing the side of my face gently. "I love you, Eileen. I'll never let anything happen to you."

When she'd uttered those words, I'd been young enough to believe that promises couldn't be broken.

Somehow, I remained cognizant that this was a dream, and I clung to her words, unwilling to let her go. I didn't have any pictures of my parents. Dreams were the only way I still got to see them. In my memory, they'd turned to shapeless figures kept alive by sheer determination, but at night, they came alive again.

"Everything will be all right," my mother whispered.

"We're going to look after you," my father added, hugging me tight, as if he knew that something bad was about to happen. Even in dreams, though, it was hard to imagine the sheer craziness of what my future was about to hold.

⊸◈⊷

I WOKE with a gasp as icy water drenched me. Screaming, I jumped to my feet, ready to fight whoever had woken me in this barbaric fashion. There was nobody to attack. Just the strange cage and at the top of it, an opening through which the water must have been pumped. I shook my fist at it, then looked around. I was no longer alone.

There were similar cages to both sides, each of them containing one person. There was someone lying in the one on my left, but to my right, a young man waved at me, a goofy smile on his face that would have seemed nice if his eyes hadn't been bloodshot with madness.

"New here?" he asked, his voice rough.

"I suppose so," I muttered, finding it a little strange to be talking to this guy without having a clue what was going on. We were caged, for goodness sake, like animals.

"Look at your arm," he said cheerily, hints of hysteria lacing his words. I almost didn't want to do it, but curiosity got the better of me. Besides, I could feel a strange tension in my left arm that I had ignored until now.

I bit back a scream when I saw what he'd been talking about. There was a machine embedded in my arm. Two metal rings, thin as elegant bracelets, were pressing into my flesh, one just above the wrist, the other a few inches below my elbow. They were *fused* with my skin somehow, and the thought of that almost made me puke. Someone had branded me with silver. How dare they! I'd come here prepared to die, but I wasn't about to be humiliated, treated like a beast.

TOUCH.

Bright green letters suddenly appeared on my arm between the two rings. They weren't painted onto my skin, but seemed to run just beneath it, as if the ink was now flowing inside my body rather than blood. This time, I really gagged.

"You better do what they say," the young man giggled. "Although, I'm sure they're going to show you what they can do."

Gingerly, I ran my right index finger over the words. They hovered there for a second, then disappeared as if they'd never been there in the first place.

"What now?" I asked when nothing happened.

"Now, the Games begin."

The man wrapped his hands around the bars of his cage and stared into the darkness. That was all there was around us. Just some bright lights illuminating the endless row of cages and darkness all around. I had no idea whether we were inside Purgatory City or somewhere else entirely.

A sharp pain made me look at my arm again.

GET READY.

"For what?" I asked. Did this machine even understand me? Could I talk to it? Or was it purely for instructions?

"The Games, silly," the young man snickered. "They're about to begin."

"What even are the Games? Could someone please tell me what's going on?"

I tried to keep the panic out of my voice, but I struggled. I'd never liked being kept in the dark, and this was an entirely new level.

"It's my third time," the man muttered. His knuckles were white from how hard he gripped the bars of his cage. "They make you do it again if you fail your probation year. Again and again and again until you're dead." He cackled madly. "This is just the beginning, sweetheart. Even if you survive, you'll have to get through an entire year inside the City. Then the tests. Then they decide whether you get to go to Eden or enter the games again. Or get killed. Some choose that rather than doing it all again." He sighed, sounding almost lucid for a second. "Maybe I should have taken that option. Too late now. Too late."

"But what are we playing?" I asked, dreading the answer.

He laughed. "We're not playing anything. We're the pawns. We do what we're told via our implants. If they tell you to go left, you go left. If they tell you to walk through fire, you walk through fire. And if they order me to kill you... well, it's all part of the Games. We don't have a say in this. We're the chess pieces in someone else's match."

I gaped at him. He couldn't be serious. All the talks of how living in Purgatory City would be amazing, how it was worth the risk of being killed at the entrance.

This was wrong. I glared at my implant, almost hoping that new words would appear so I could disobey them.

TOUCH YOUR RIGHT EAR.

I stared at the words on my arm. Touch my ear? I stared at the crazy guy in the cage nearby. No one else was talking. If they heard me, they didn't comment or maybe they were all passed out. I'd gotten by for years now on my instincts and they were screaming for me to be hesitant with the guy in the cage. He was good-looking, young. But he'd clearly lost his wits. I had to look out for myself in whatever happened here. I couldn't be worrying about the crazy man in the other cage.

Even if he was blond, and I'd always been a sucker for blond bad boys. Was he that or just bonkers?

I touched my ear. That seemed easy enough. Of course, if my ear suddenly cut off my finger, I was going to regret listening to the instructions.

"Good job." A male's voice blasted into my ear, and I jumped. "Hold on. Sorry. Volume was turned way up. This better?"

I swallowed. Oh my, I was about to be as crazed as the boy in the cage. I was hearing voices in my ear.

"No." The man sighed. "You're not crazy, and you can answer me. In fact, you'd better. Take it as a direction. I can put it on your wristband, or you can just do it. Are you going to be difficult?"

"I... I can hear you. Volume's fine."

Blondie groaned. "Oh, of course. Yours talks to you. Mine won't say a word to me in a year, but you? Sure. They speak to you."

I ignored him as the man in my ear spoke again. "Great. So, you're Eileen. I see that here. And I bet you're confused. That's normal. Let me start from the beginning. You can call me Tim. I am your Guide. You and me? We're going to get you probation in Purgatory City so that you can move on."

I needed a guide? I pulled my knees up to my forehead. All right, I needed to breathe. This all seemed like too much, but it was happening, and I had to deal. I'd chosen this. I'd lined up for the chance.

Blondie sighed. "It's a lot. And the Guides are assholes. Mine sucked. It's his fault I'm in round three here."

"Oh, I can hear what you do now. Ignore him. That's Kenneth, they call him Kenny. He might be on his way to execution. You want to ignore everything he says to you and pay attention to me."

I scowled. All right, they could see me, and now random voice Tim wanted me to pay no attention to the person trying to help me and explain things to listen to him just because he somehow got access to my ear? No, that wasn't going to happen.

"You don't say much or maybe you don't trust me. That's fine. All I can tell you is that I have as much invested in this as you do. First things first, you need to earn the right to get out of that cage."

I cleared my throat. "How do I do that?"

"By learning to do what you're told. The stakes are too high for you to fail me."

I grimaced at my arm, hoping that there wasn't a secret camera under my skin. I wouldn't have put it past them. How was he even talking in my head? Had they put an implant in there, too? The thought of that made my skin crawl. Not just because it was creepy to think that they'd done it all without my permission, but also because of the technology that made it all possible. The potential of it. Out in the Blastlands, people were dying because they didn't have clean water. There was no fuel for the few remaining cars that would have still worked and barely any electricity. And here I was with stuff embedded into my body that was probably worth more than my life. Worth more money than my entire family had ever owned. Crazy.

"Who are you?" I asked, feeling a little rebellious.

Probably a bad idea. "Why do you think you can order me around?"

Suddenly, I was on my knees, burying my head in my hands as agonizing pain crashed into me from all sides. My skin felt like it was being peeled off my flesh in long strips, while my head was close to exploding. It only lasted seconds, but when it was over, my cheeks were streaked with tears and my throat hurt from screaming.

"That's who I am," Tim said calmly. "I bought you, you're mine. I have the right to make you do what I say and punish you if you don't. Do you understand?"

I didn't reply. He'd hurt me just to prove a point. I looked down at my bare arms and legs, almost expecting them to be drenched in blood. Nothing. It had all been in my mind. Whatever they'd done to me must have given them the ability to make me feel pain without my body suffering any damage. How convenient for them.

"Are you ready to prove your worth?" Tim asked.

Again, I stayed quiet. He could kiss my ass. I was not going to jump for him like a monkey.

"Take off your shirt."

Instinctively, I crossed my arms over my chest. I was still wearing the same clothes I had arrived in, tattered and old, but good at concealing my body. If you wanted to survive as a woman in the Blastlands, you had to make sure not to look attractive in the slightest. I never wore anything but baggy clothes and didn't go near a comb to untangle my hair. Sometimes it felt like an insult to my mother, who'd always taken care that we all looked presentable, no matter the poor quality of our clothes. It was better than being raped and killed, though.

"I'd do what he ordered you to do," crazy blond guy said. I glared at him.

"You don't even know what he's said," I snapped.

"They always make you do something you don't want at the beginning." He grinned. "I'll guess from the way you're clutching your shirt, he wants you to strip?"

I sighed. "Yes. So turn around. I don't want you looking, Kenny." I glared at him. "He told me your name."

The crazy yet somewhat hot guy turned around in his cage. "If he's so chatty, maybe you could ask him why I don't have anyone in my ear and haven't for days."

I wasn't going to ask this Tim that. If anything, I was going to keep my interaction with this person who claimed he'd paid for me to a minimum. We'd use each other for whatever he got out of this, and then move on with our lives when I got out of Purgatory and got on with the real agenda, which was getting to Paradise.

That was where I was headed.

I took off my shirt and threw it aside. I was pretty. Everyone had always told me that, and I knew it could be a commodity. If I'd stayed where I was, prostitution was a viable, legal option for some women. You had to be twenty-one to apply for those jobs, and at nineteen, I had preferred the thought of this to that. Still, I'd never discarded my clothes in public with strangers watching. My boyfriend when I was younger had only seen me with my shirt off once.

My cheeks heated as I waited there. "All right, Tim. Alight if I call you Tim? I'm shirtless. Now what?"

Silence met my query for a second. "Good job. That was to see if you'd listen, even when things were hard. You can put your shirt back on. And by the way, I'm being nice to you. Your buddy Kenny over there had to kill someone as his first instruction. He hesitated but did it, if I recall correctly. Consider yourself lucky all I did was ask you to strip."

He wanted me to be grateful. "It's always that way, right? Even here, at the end of the world with aliens running our lives? Men are violent, women are sexual objects. Don't consider yourself original."

Kenny laughed, a loud sound, as he threw his head back. "Oh, they're going to love you. Didn't I mention it? That guy in your ear? He's one of those aliens. Don't expect sympathy from them. I've never seen one of their females, so my guess would be they're barefoot and pregnant at home. Can I turn around now?"

I put my shirt back on, waiting for a response from Timothy, but didn't get one. This had only started, this strange voyage I'd signed up for, and already I knew that the anticipation of what would happen next was going to be as difficult as anything.

"The door to your cage is going to open. When I tell you to, step out of it. Failure to do so will result in a jolt."

I could almost hear him reading from a manual. Tell the prisoner this, tell the prisoner that.

For now, I would listen to his instructions. It was the only way to learn his weaknesses. But when the time came, I'd be the first to get rid of that horrid implant and make my destiny my own again. I'd come to Purgatory City to spend a while in servitude before moving on to a better life. I hadn't signed up for this.

[2]

He left me waiting for several minutes before he finally told me to leave the cage. I did so slowly, almost expecting it to be a trap.

"Walk straight ahead, don't look back," Tim said in my ear. Or maybe my head. It was hard to decide where his voice was exactly.

"But it's dark," I protested, although I kept walking. "I won't be able to see where I'm going."

"Walk," was all Timothy had to say.

I bit back a reply and did as he said, putting one foot in front of the other, even when the light of the cages disappeared and all that remained around me was darkness. The ground was soft, like sand, but I didn't trust it to stay that way. With every step, I tested the ground, searched for stones that would make me trip.

When I'd been walking for at least five minutes, I dared to ask Tim how much longer it would be.

"Keep walking. If you ask another stupid question, you'll regret it."

His voice was harsh and cold. He was no longer keeping

up the pretense of being nice and on my side. I didn't really believe what Kenny had said. Tim couldn't be one of the aliens who had invaded our planet two decades before. Those couldn't even speak. Not our language, anyway, and nobody had ever managed to make sense of the clicking sounds they made. Not that they bothered trying to communicate with us. They wanted our resources, our water most of all, and they took it with whatever force was necessary.

No, this was something else, something much more sophisticated. The Kragatons were all about brute force. They didn't use strategy or finesse. All they relied on was their superior strength and technology. This, however, was different. A game in which we desperate refugees had become the chess pieces. They were exploiting our hopes for their own entertainment. If this really were the Kragatons, I'd take off my shirt again and eat it.

A light flickered in the distance, reminding me of a street lamp. Not that many of those were still working, only the ones relying on solar power. The others had been switched off right at the beginning, when power became too valuable to waste on illuminating our streets.

"Head toward the light," Tim instructed. I was kind of grateful for it. Aimlessly walking in the dark made the whole situation even more frightening.

I increased my pace and hurried toward the light as fast as I dared without tripping in the darkness. A light could mean hope. Or danger. Not to mention the last light situation landed me in a cage. Luckily, I was an optimistic person.

When I got close enough to see that it wasn't a streetlamp but some kind of small electronic flare stuck in the ground, a large shadow behind it made me stop. A house. Well, more of a shed. One story with no windows, a metal door and a flat roof.

"Go inside," Tim ordered. "This will be your base. They'll come to take it soon, so you need to get ready to defend it."

"They? Who?" I asked.

"Other players. This place may not look like much, but it's a vital strategic resource. You'll see in the morning."

"It's night?" I was a little confused. It had been early morning when I'd entered Purgatory City, and I didn't think I'd been unconscious for this long. I'd put the darkness around me down to being inside somewhere, a massive space with a roof blocking out all the light.

"In a way," he said mysteriously. "We don't base night and day on the sun. It's too wasteful to spend all night sleeping. We've shortened night and lengthened day. More productivity."

That sounded like a system set up to fail. Sleep was important. I loved sleep, personally, although I never got enough. Not with the threats of living in the Blastlands forcing me to be always aware of my surroundings. I'd hoped that would change in Purgatory City. Well, seemed like it was going to be the opposite. I entered the little building.

"Eileen, you're up." The voice in my ear said, his calm manner belaying what he was actually saying, that the other players had come and now I had to... fight them?

I caught my breath in my throat. "I didn't sign up for this."

"You did, actually." Was that bastard laughing at me?

If there was any justice in the world—and I knew there wasn't—I would get revenge for this some day. Just because I knew how things went in the world, didn't mean I had personal experience doing them. I didn't have the slightest clue how to defend an area. I'd never had to do so in my life. We just sort of existed where I'd lived. Why would anyone want what little I possessed when they had just the same amount of nothing? It was equal that way, I supposed.

Three figures appeared in the doorway. It was hard to see, but my terrified and tired brain at least allowed me to figure out they were male. More men than women tried to get into this nonsense. None of us had known what to expect, but since this was clearly some sort of death trap for the amusement of whoever Tim and his ilk were, it might help to have physical strength.

I held up my hands. "The man in my ear says I have to defend this place. I'm new and..."

"And you don't have the slightest idea how." The tallest of the group, the guy in the center, took a step toward me. "That's okay. None of us did in the beginning. I'm not going to hurt you unless you make me. For now. I'm Clay. I run this group. Sort of." He took another step toward me. "Your controller told you to defend this place. Well, you can do that. You can do that by letting me come in with my friends here to speak to you. There are more of us than you. One way to do what the alien wants is to listen carefully to what he is saying to you. Defend it from the other players." He held up his hands. "There's no need to do that if I'm not trying to take it from you. Right? I'm not here to take. I'm here to share. That's a defensive move, right? Is he saying otherwise to you?"

No, jackass in my ear had gone silent, which was good because Clay continued to speak. "We're the A players. We win. We listen. We do what they say, and we don't die... that's how we win. You can do that, too, new girl, if you play nicely with us." He was close enough to touch me, and he put out his hand like he wanted to shake. "I'm Clay. But I told you that. So how about you tell me your name—"

"Hey," Kenny shouted as he ran in the room. "They let me out and—fuck—the yes men have found you."

Clay winced. "I see you've met the biggest pain in my ass. Still alive, Ken?"

"Eileen," I managed to get out to both of them. It was going to be important to remember that, to keep in mind who I was, as I tried to figure out where the hell to go from here. In my ear, Timothy, my so-called alien controller who had bought me, didn't say a word. That was a small relief.

Kenny shook his head. "I've got one in my ear again. Calling himself Fred. Well, Fred, since we know you're as much a Fred as I am one of the clicking creatures you control, I don't care how much you zap me, I'm pretty much immune."

Clay looked over his shoulder at the two men by the door. "You might as well come in, guys. As you can see, we once again have to deal with dingbat here. And—Eileen—I think she's smart enough to know how to stay alive."

There were two things I already understood. Clay was in charge, and as gorgeous as he was with his bright blue eyes I could see even in the near darkness, he wasn't a benevolent leader. He had as much to lose as any of us. Kenny was still alive, even after he'd clearly been a problem to everyone. They both had things to teach me.

I stepped back and forced my body to relax. Not that I was feeling relaxed inside, but I didn't want them to think I was scared of them. Showing fear made you prey. I wasn't going to be their prey. I was going to become one of them, if that was what it took to survive. I was a survivor, always had been, and that wasn't going to change now.

"Come in, make yourselves at home," I said with a smirk.

The cabin was empty, so there wasn't anywhere for them to sit other than on the dusty ground.

Clay grinned and pushed past me before sitting down in a corner. Took me a second, but it dawned on me that it was the best strategic position in the cabin; he could see both me and the door, and nobody could surprise him from behind. Clever boy. Not that he was a boy. He had to be in his late twenties, unless the struggle to survive had aged him.

Kenny threw himself onto the ground at the back, stretching out with something that reminded me of a purr. He looked like he was about to fall asleep. The maternal instinct in me wanted to cover him with a non-existent blanket, but I pushed that away. He was crazy, we were all in danger, and I still hadn't got a clue what was going on.

The other two men entered the cabin, taking position on either side of the door. The light was too dim to make out much, so I stepped toward them until I could see their features. Their eyes were exactly the same. Bright green with turquoise specks around the iris. That was where the similarities ended, though. The one on the left had dark brown hair that fell onto his shoulders in gentle curls, framing a face so clean and pretty that it didn't seem to be long into this world. The man next to him was the opposite. His face was covered in scars, some so thick that it was hard to tell how he may have looked before. His head was shaved, exposing yet another scar running all the way from his right eyebrow to the nape of his neck. What the fuck had happened to him? How had he survived whatever had done this to his face?

"Meet X and Y," Clay said from behind me. "They're brothers. Neither of them talks much, so don't expect to have long conversations with them. My theory is that their handlers forbade them to speak."

Both men stared at me, not saying a word. I felt a little uncomfortable under their intense gaze, but I kept looking straight ahead, taking both of them in. Their bodies were athletic and lithe, perfect for surviving in whatever cruel game we were playing. I bet they could outrun me without even breaking a sweat.

Suddenly, the guy on the left shot forward, wrapping his hands around my throat. We tumbled to the ground, my back hitting a sharp stone. I would have screamed if his hands hadn't prevented me from breathing. I struggled against his grip, but he shifted around until he was sitting on top of me, using his body weight to subdue me. I tried to pry his hands off, but he was too strong. No matter how much I scratched him, he didn't let go.

Black spots began to shimmer in front of my eyes. Now would have been a really good moment for Tim to resurface. There were sounds in the background, but my eyes started to buzz, droning out the voices. I was becoming too weak to struggle.

I was dying.

He was killing me.

"Oh no, he's not."

Tim's voice rang through my brain, loud and clear. A moment later, pain filled my skull and my vision disappeared, followed by a loud bang. The hands around my throat vanished, and I drew in a ragged breath, almost too weak to breathe.

Then there was silence. I still couldn't see, but nobody spoke to tell me what was happening. Time seemed to pass quickly but there was nothing I could do about it. My throat hurt like hell, and my lungs were burning. Why had that bastard tried to kill me? Had it been their plan all along?

Slowly, the darkness receded a little.

"Can you stand up?" Tim asked in my head after what felt like forever.

I doubted it. I couldn't even blink my eyes open. I was weak as a baby, unable to move, unable to speak.

"Seems I need to work on this defense tech," he muttered, almost as if to himself, which was kind of ironic seeing that it was him in my brain and not the other way round. "If it leaves you unable to run after deployment, it's of no use."

None of what he said made sense. I wish I could have asked him, but even swallowing was almost impossible. I wrenched my eyes open and groaned. Okay. I wasn't being attacked anymore. The one who had been doing it was across the space, holding his head, and I clearly had done something to him, even if I couldn't remember what that was.

"Interesting," Kenny chuckled, his voice crazed once again. "I didn't expect that. You were out for an entire hour."

Clay groaned. "Neither did I. Nice trick, Eileen."

Sounds of footsteps were followed by someone putting a hand on my forehead.

"Wow, you're burning up. What did those bastards do to you?"

"She's a new generation," a new voice said. It had to be X or Y. "Sorry, lass. I had to know if they'd modified you. Only major threats reveal the tech they've implanted in you. Guess this is our lucky day."

My throat hurt, and Tim wasn't commenting. For all the tech that was apparently installed inside of me, healing me was clearly not a priority. They didn't want me dead yet?

Great. I was on board with that, but he could have thrown in a throat lozenge, and I'd have been thrilled with that, too.

Not that we'd had any for years. I rubbed my throat, and Clay bent over to hand me some hot tea. They must have brought supplies with them. I gladly took the mug.

The man grimaced. "Sorry about your throat. He wouldn't have killed you. I mean, you would have passed out, but unless he was instructed to kill, X wasn't going to do that."

I leaned forward. "It was a dick move. Coming in here like you're friendly, like you want to be some kind of big instructor and friend in this hellhole, and going for my throat? That is really low. Although, maybe I should be thanking you because your little test did teach me more than anything else could have."

The fire they'd lit outside the cabin crackled as Y threw a stick into it. After X's apology, those two had gone back to being silent. Clay had been right about them. They didn't talk much. I preferred it that way.

Ken laughed, sitting back on his elbows. "No heroes in here, Eileen. I don't like your name. I'm going to come up with something else. I'll let you know when I decide what it is."

I'd never cared for nicknames. "Don't hurt yourself trying."

Clay sat with his elbows on his knees, looking between us. "Don't decide he's better than us, Eileen. And, yeah, I like your name just fine."

I really didn't give a shit and opened my mouth to tell him so, but my throat was on fire, and I decided not to expend the energy answering.

He must have taken it as a sign that he should keep talking, which was unfortunate since I pretty much thought if I could kill anyone right now it would be Clay and his crew. "Anything we learned about surviving in here, we learned from Ken and his old crew."

Kenny threw a stick at Clay. "All of whom are dead now. So you might want to rethink whatever lessons it is you think that I taught you." He smiled. "I wasn't looking to teach you anything. I'm sorry if you thought I was some kind of mentor."

There were a ton of undertones going on here. They'd had some kind of relationship before Kenny went... nuts. But none of that mattered because when it came down to it, I had tech they wanted. I needed to know all the things I was carrying, and that wasn't going to come from the four guys here—no matter how hot they were. No, I wanted Tim to tell me before I got choked again. If I knew what I was carrying, what they'd put in my body, I could defend myself, and that was what they wanted, that was what I was supposed to show them. That simply meant I had to speak to Tim. In the morning. I'd had enough. For now.

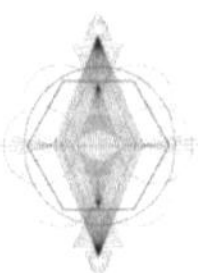

3

I was almost surprised to wake up at all. Somehow, I wouldn't have been shocked if one of the men had slit my throat while I slept, either to take out the competition or to get whatever technology was in my body.

I cleared my throat and pain immediately shot up and down my neck. I probably had bruises all over. I was going to kill X when I got the chance. I didn't owe any of them anything. I was going to survive. Even if that seemed unlikely. I'd...make it happen.

I sat up, suppressing a groan. Everything hurt. Kenny was sleeping in one corner, Y in another. The other two guys were on either side of me, close enough to touch.

"Tim?" I whispered, holding my arm close to my face. Was there a microphone in the thing they'd put in my arm? Or was there one somewhere else, in my head maybe, like the speaker through which I heard Tim? A shiver ran down my back at the thought of all that metal inside of me. I hadn't even had a tattoo before I entered Purgatory City, and now I was full of body modifications that I hadn't chosen myself.

"Good morning," Tim said happily, his voice booming through my head. I groaned. He was far too happy for my taste.

"What have you done to me?" I asked, ignoring his cheerful mood. "What happened last night?"

"Shhhushhh!" Kenny muttered, barely awake. I ignored him. This was more important than his beauty sleep.

"Made you better," Tim replied, still annoyingly happy. "Improved your feeble human body to withstand the dangers ahead. Sadly, there was nothing we could do about your intelligence or your emotional immaturity."

I growled at my wrist, wishing that I could see him, whoever or whatever he was.

"What was that yesterday?" I asked again.

"Prosynchronic wave. A new technology we've been exploring. It's existed as a large-scale weapon for decades, but nobody has ever managed to make it small enough to fit into a wearable device before. You're the first to have this implant, so consider yourself famous. You'll go down in the history books as either the first person to have lived or to have died with prosynchronic technology attached to their nervous system."

I shuddered, despite not knowing how to defend an overall area, I actually had a pretty good idea what to do about taking care of my own person. I had no idea what those waves were, but it didn't sound pleasant. Weapons. I'd learned to shoot a gun, but of course there was limited ammunition in this world, so my father had insisted on me perfecting hand-to-hand combat instead. He'd been a large man, which meant I was well-trained in taking down bigger opponents than me. Still, I'd never considered my body to be a weapon. Until now.

"How does it work?" I whispered.

"It's too complicated to even begin to explain it to you. It only activates when you're about to pass out, or if you have a severely bleeding wound. It disrupts the brain waves of any human in a three-meter radius, incapacitating them for at least thirty seconds. That should give you long enough to escape. Of course, we didn't expect it to affect you like it did. We're going to have to tweak the tech."

Tweak the tech? I cleared my throat, and Clay rolled over, muttering something. For people who were always apparently ready to be at war with each other, they managed to sleep very well. Deeper than I'd ever slept in my life, that was for sure. Or at least since my parents had been gone. X, my would-be assassin, snored lightly.

"How are you going to do that? Test it on someone else or on me?"

A light laughter moved through me. It was low, and would be sexy, if it wasn't connected to a faceless alien bent on using me like some kind of lab rat. "On you, darling."

I already didn't care for that endearment. "How do you propose to do that?"

"Like this."

The world went white.

⋯⋆⋯

I woke up with a groan that was only made worse by the fact that my throat still hurt. The cage was once again around me, and I couldn't say that I liked it any better this time than I had the last. My head pounded, and my ears rang. I would have done anything in the world for a cup of coffee, but I doubted there was one to be found.

I got up on my knees. What had I learned? Not much. Just that they could knock me out, reset my tech, and I'd end up back in this cage without so much as by my leave. Fuck. This. Shit. I sighed. This fucking sucked.

Tears I didn't want to shed trailed down my cheeks, and I pushed them away.

"Eileen?"

Timothy's voice bounced around in my head, and I almost answered. This time, however, it brought with it an image. Greyish skin, soft, almost human features that were just slightly too wide. Yet, kind blue eyes.

A hand on my forehead. *I know you'll never believe this, but I don't want to do these things to you.*

"Eileen, can you hear me?"

I blinked the dream away, not even sure what I was seeing. "Yes, Timothy, I can hear you. Despite the brain damage I'm sure you've inflicted on me."

The sound of his laughter made me want to throw something. "Well, that's good. Haven't lost your sense of humor. Okay. You can leave the cage. Go on outside. Let's see if we can find any new people to play with."

That sounded like hell, but seeing as I had no choice and wasn't staying in that cage, I got up and sluggishly took myself back outside again. Apparently, the only way I was going to get any sleep was going to be when Timothy needed to reset my tech.

"You're back." Kenny jumped out of a tree, holding onto his ear and nearly landing in front of me. Daytime certainly made things easier. "Hold on. The alien is talking to me. Yeah... okay. I'm supposed to be doing something else. Want to come with me? I need to go see how long I can hold my breath under water. You can watch."

I blinked. Sure. Why the fuck not?

"Where are the others? What happened after I passed out?"

Kenny grinned, his eyes full of his usual craziness. "No idea. I woke up in a cage, just like you. Maybe the others got out of the way, maybe they passed out, maybe they're dead. Everything's possible in this game. Never trust what you see and never, ever think that you're safe."

He cackled loudly. Damn. If there was anyone around, they surely knew now that we existed. I didn't trust Tim's technology to keep me safe. He'd not even told me what he'd done to me this time. Had they added new things to me? Or just changed the old ones? More waves with names I couldn't even remember?

After pulling on my clothes so I could adjust them, I looked up and down my body, checking for scars or marks, but there was nothing new. Just the terrible display in my left arm, branded in there, part of me and yet not at all.

"Go with him," Tim encouraged me. "There are some others heading in your direction, they'll be perfect to try your new skills on."

"Care to explain what skills those might be?" I growled, wishing that Tim was in front of me so I could punch him.

"You'll find out. Now go and follow that boy before he manages to drown himself."

"I thought that was the point?"

Tim chuckled. "Trust me, we handlers are very much invested in our charges' wellbeing. If you die, there are consequences for us, too. Not as dramatic as death, but still, bad enough that we try to avoid that. So we play the game, just like you, aiming to win."

"I don't care about winning," I snapped. "I just want to survive."

He laughed softly. "Don't we all. Now hurry, or do you need a reminder of what I can do if you don't follow my instructions?"

I glared at my arm but started to run after Kenny, who'd already made it quite far. He may not have been in good condition mentally, but his body was in top shape. He could easily outrun me, if he wanted, clearly. Same with the other men. They were all stronger and faster than me, so I had to rely on my mind to get me out of this. For now, I was going to play along, but as soon as there was any chance of escape, I'd take it. By now, I would be happy to return to the Blastlands. At least there I had control over myself, my body, my mind. No alien sitting inside my brain. No strange game being played without my permission.

We finally stopped in a clearing with a giant lake that seemed to take up most of the horizon as far as I could see. We weren't the only ones there. There were lots of people in it. Diving, jumping, swimming to the edge and back again.

"This is Bandit Lake. I don't know that it's really called that, but that's what we call it. I've never had a voice in my head correct that title, so either they don't give a shit or they call it that, too." Kenny took off his shirt. I gawked and then pretended I hadn't. Although he looked thin in his clothes— or maybe lean was the right word—Kenny was built like a statue made of rock. We were all starved coming out of the Blastland, and most men I knew never got the chance to put on muscle because they didn't get enough protein. But someone had fed Kenny, and he was... hot.

Crazy and hot. But also somehow the one who had taught Clay, X, and Y how to survive here, like an old leader. I couldn't make heads nor tails of him. I wasn't sure I should want to, except that he'd yet to leave me alone, always seeming to want to help. Had he really been put back in the cage or was he just saying that?

"Is your alien telling you to swim?" he questioned me,

seemingly unaware of the fact that I stood there gawking at his bare chest like I'd never seen one before.

I shook my head. "No, Tim told me to come with you but not to swim."

"Well, like I said, this is Bandit Lake. We're sent here a lot. Training. Maybe to drown someone." He looked around. "So, you might want to watch yourself in the water if that were to be told to you. You can be swimming around toning your body for the amusement of the creatures watching us, and boom—someone is trying to end your life."

I swallowed. "Seems like it's that a lot."

"This is Purgatory City, beautiful. And Purgatory can so quickly become Hellfire and Brimstone."

I shivered at his words. "Did you make that up yourself?"

"Maybe." He winked at me. "Maybe not."

Timothy sighed. "He didn't. That's an old saying in there. Older than even he knows. But I'll tell you what? I think it would be great to see how you can handle yourself in the water. I don't see any kill orders around me, so I think you should be safe. Go for a swim. Take your clothes off. This time of year, it's not too cold."

"You say that like you've been in the lake yourself."

Kenny shook his head. "I've never seen anyone talk to their controller like you do. For most of us it's yes or no, or we just do it or don't do it. You're always in conversation with the bastard."

With that being said, he threw himself into the water and started to swim. He must have been given instructions to hold his breath, because he seemed like he moved with determination, a person with a destination in mind.

I took off my clothes slowly. It was bad enough knowing Tim watched, but I didn't need strangers who might set out to kill me watching my naked form either. Or whoever was witnessing this with Tim.

"Do you guys get your jollies off doing this?" I asked him.

He was quiet for a second. "No. You're a beautiful human girl, but no. I promise you that. And... you can talk to me all you like. Screw Kenny. His controller talks to no one. He's just jealous."

I didn't know what to say to any of that, so I dived into the water. Thank God I'd learned to swim when I was a little girl. What would they have done otherwise?

The water was surprisingly warm, balmy almost. The perfect temperature to stay in for a while without freezing to death. I dived down, enjoying the feeling of water tousling my hair. Almost as if someone was running their fingers through it.

Tim hadn't said anything about where I should swim, so I gathered that this was my own decision. Finally. It seemed like a small mercy to be able to decide for myself for once, even if it was only such a small thing.

I stayed away from the people at the other end of the lake and followed Kenny, who was quickly swimming away, instead. I got glimpses of his muscled arms diving out of the water like dolphins, propelling him forward at a speed I'd never be able to match. I hadn't swum in ages, and I was already feeling the strain in my arms and shoulders.

Still, feeling clean for the first time in forever was amazing. I'd been dirty and dusty ever since I could remember, and I doubted I was going to get a chance to wash or have a shower anytime soon, so I was going to make this count.

I began to swim faster, putting as much strength into my strokes as possible. I wasn't going to catch up with Kenny, but maybe I could get to him before he drowned himself. His controller had to be as crazy as Kenny seemed to be. Maybe that was the cause of his weirdness? Could a controller's personality somehow filter through to the controlled? I surely hoped not. Hearing Tim in my head was bad enough, I really didn't need to take on any of his aspects, too.

"I like your style," Tim said, as if he'd been listening to my thoughts. Which he probably had. "Our people swim in a very different way."

I had to stop in order to speak without swallowing a whole lot of water. "What do you even look like? Are you humanoid? You know, with arms and legs?"

He chuckled. "Wouldn't you like to know..."

"Yes, I would, actually."

"Would it truly make a difference if I looked like a slug or some kind of octopus with tentacles? It's not as if you're ever going to see me."

A pang of regret fluttered in his voice. As if he was sad about that. And why did my own heart echo that emotion? Surely just because I wanted to know my enemy. That was what he was, I had to remember that. The enemy. Just because he had a pretty voice and didn't incessantly torture me, that didn't mean that he was my friend. I needed to stay wary.

I took a deep breath and dived, ending the conversation. The lake wasn't very deep, maybe three meters or so, but too murky to see much. I swam to the very bottom, touching the muddy ground with my toes. It was beautifully quiet down there. No people, no voices in my head, no problems. I wished I could stay under for a while longer. The world above the surface was full of problems and danger.

The slight burn in my lungs dispelled the fantasy of

staying underwater. Unless Tim could modify me and give me gills... but no, better not. As handy as they would be, having gills would be a little too weird.

I swam back to the surface and breathed in deep before I sunk down for a second, losing my way. The taste of murky water filled my mouth as I swallowed far too much of it. Strangely enough, the yucky taste made me feel alive. I pushed back up to the surface. Maybe I was going crazy like Kenny.

I tread water, turning and searching for Kenny. He was nowhere to be seen. Maybe he was doing his experiment already. Fuck. I shouldn't have dawdled. Who knew whether his controller would tell Kenny to resurface before it was too late.

"Kenny!" I shouted as loud as I could. Several heads turned toward me. Damn. A guy and a girl stared at me from the other end of the lake, then dived into the water in beautiful synchrony. This was bad news. I'd attracted attention, the one thing I should have avoided.

Panic spread through my chest, and my heart started beating faster.

"A kill order has been issued," Tim alerted me, his voice frantic. "Get out of the water!"

But... Kenny! I still couldn't see him. I couldn't leave him, not if he was in danger. Maybe the kill order wasn't just for me, but for him, too. I dived, blinking fast, trying to see, but the water was too murky.

"Go now!" Tim shouted, making my head hurt. The urgency in his words made me follow his command, turning toward the bank closest to me. I stayed underwater until my lungs ached, but even when I resurfaced, I refused to look back. Knowing how close the two were to me wouldn't make a difference. I had to get out of here and run.

My muscles screamed at me to stop, to slow down, but I ignored the pain. The bank of the lake was so close. Just a few more strokes...

Hands clawed at my shoulders, pushing me down underwater, drowning me.

4

I fought, hard. There were two of them and one of me. My hands, my feet. I could feel Tim in my head yelling, but I couldn't listen to him, not when I had to survive. How much time had passed? I wasn't sure. Five seconds. Ten?

The same surge that had shoved X off blasted through me but it didn't seem to work. For a second, my two attackers jerked back but not the way it had done in the cabin. Things must have been different because of the water. My lungs burned. I could fight on land, but this? Terror filled me. I was going to die.

Suddenly the two were ripped backward. I surfaced on a gasp. Nausea roiled through me as I puked up the water I'd ingested. My stomach roiled. What was happening? I couldn't think through the ringing in my ears. My eyes burned. I coughed, hard. Arms came around my waist, hauling me toward the shore.

I didn't know who it was, and I struggled, but I had no fight in me. I could hardly breathe between gasping and coughing. Everything hurt.

"Easy," Clay spoke against my ear. "I'm not going to hurt you. I promise you that, and the two that went after you are being dealt with."

I lifted my head just in time to see X twist the guy's head back in such a way that he broke his neck. I would have gasped if I'd had any air to spare. Y held the woman who'd attacked me, her neck hung in a funny way, her eyes unseeing. He dropped her body into the lake.

Next to me on the ground, Clay put his hand on my back. "This is us making up for yesterday. Consider us even."

I stared at him. I couldn't talk yet, but I wouldn't let myself cry. Kenny swam up to the scene, eyeing it, before his gaze caught mine. "I guess we had a kill order. You okay, Brown Eyes?"

I shook my head. "I guess so. Thanks to them."

X and Y—I really needed to learn their names—waded out of the water toward us. "You okay, lass?"

X asked me the question, and I nodded. "Thanks."

I still had yet to hear Y speak, but he patted my head when he walked away from me, sinking to the ground. We all sat there, the five of us, saying nothing at all. What was there to say? Two strangers had been ordered by the aliens in their head to kill me, and I'd been unable to defend myself at all.

"I think there's a problem with the tech in the water, Tim." Just in case he'd missed the obvious problem when I'd almost been drowned.

Clay shifted to stare at me. "Do you talk to yours? And fuck, we have to get you some clothes."

"She does. It's so lit." Kenny laughed. "This place got a lot more interesting with you in, Brown Eyes. Look how mature I'm being about you being naked. Here..." He pulled off a shirt, and I smiled at him as I put it on fast.

Brown Eyes. That was apparently going to me by name, since he'd decided he didn't like mine. I supposed it could be worse. My eyes were brown. He could have come up with something much worse—like Drowned Rat. Or Naked Girl. That was pretty much how I felt right then, and Tim had nothing at all to say.

When nobody said anything, I turned to Clay, a thousand questions burning on my tongue. "Where have you been? What happened at the hut? I was back in a cage, but you were all gone..."

He sighed. "You blacked out without warning, but before we could even make sure you were all right, the aliens came."

I stared at him. "Wait, the aliens actually appeared? In the flesh? Walking on Earth?"

He grinned at my confusion. "No, obviously not. No one's ever seen them here. They send drones, and those weird looking robots to do their dirty work. They surrounded us, guns everywhere, and then one of the big androids picked you up and carried you off. There was no way we could have stopped them." He nodded toward Kenny, who was trying to squeeze the water out of his hair. "Kenny followed them, since he's the best at staying hidden. The rest of us stayed at the hut to prevent anyone else from taking it over. A base like that is precious."

"Not that we have it anymore," X grumbled. I showed him a questioning look, and he sighed. "We were overrun. Twenty or so people at once. We didn't stand a chance."

His brother nodded with a wistful look in his eyes but stayed quiet.

"Eileen, you need to leave, now," Tim suddenly said in

my head, his voice urgent. "Things are happening, you're in danger."

"What kind of danger?"

The guys all looked at me in confusion, but I ignored them.

"Hurry, there's not much time. Players have grouped together, and they're taking out anyone who's not part of their gang. Get up and run!"

The last bit was a shout so loud that it made my ears ring. I squeezed my eyes shut, waiting for the pain to stop.

"What's wrong?" Kenny asked, all craziness gone from his tone.

"We need to go," I muttered, still trying to get rid of Tim's voice echoing around my head. I really had to tell him never to shout in there.

"No, *you* need to go, alone," Tim protested. "I don't know on which side their controllers are. They might simply be biding their time and letting others do the dirty work first. You're not safe with them. Don't say anything, just get up and run."

I studied the men surrounding me. Even though I hardly knew them, I couldn't imagine any of them killing me. Not even after seeing X and Y dispatching the two swimmers. But then, they were puppets controlled by the strings of their masters, just like me. I knew how much it could hurt when the alien decided to inflict pain. No, I didn't want to think of Tim as an alien. That made him being inside my head even creepier.

"I need to go," I stuttered, stumbling to my feet. I realized only now that being wet in the t-shirt was as bad as being in my underwear. My nipples were almost poking through the fabric. As much as I wanted to cover myself, it was too late for that. They'd all seen me. And Clay had had his hand on my back. My cheeks burned at the thought. Fuck.

"Eileen!" Tim yelled. "You need to listen to me and not dawdle anymore."

"Is anyone else getting an alert for danger?" Clay looked at Kenny, then X and Y. The last two shook their heads, and Kenny shrugged. With the tension between those two, I doubted Kenny would share if he was getting alerted.

Still, Tim wanted me to go, so I was going. "Bye, guys, thank you."

They all nodded, and I didn't miss the way the four of them stared at my body. We were all aware that I was pretty much naked in front of them. I'd never been an exhibitionist, and if I really thought about this, I was all but nude in front of a lot more than these four men here. No, there were huge amounts of aliens and maybe even people looking at me now.

"Wait." Y got to his feet. His voice was scratchy, like he was hoarse, and I wondered if that was permanent, or if he was sick in some way. He pulled his shirt off and handed it to me. "It's wet, but when it dries, it'll offer you some kind of... I don't know... covering."

I took his offering in my hand. Did he just carry them around? Did he have a whole bag of shirts? He was shirtless now so maybe not any more. Or who knew, maybe he had a stash somewhere. "You might get cold."

"I'll find another shirt." He gripped his head. "Sorry. Too much talking."

"His handler doesn't like it when he's chatty," Kenny supplied. "They've all got their sick fascinations. Take it. Y isn't altruistic. Trust me on that."

Y rolled his eyes at Kenny, and I nodded. "Thank you. If I can make it up to you someday, I will."

With that, I took off running. I didn't even know where I was going, but it was what Tim had told me to do.

They all had their sick fascinations? I looked over my shoulder, feeling really alone for the first time since I'd woken up in the cage. What was Tim's? I had no way of knowing yet. No one else was around, and I didn't see others tearing off to hide. I chewed on my lip. Maybe Tim's was that he didn't want me around other people? But then again, if I hadn't been, I'd be dead, so... what was going on here? Did I just have to trust him? I had no choice. I was physically out of control of my own person.

"Are you okay?" Tim's voice was soft. "I thought I was going to lose you."

"What would happen if you did? Would you just get assigned a new toy and move on? Or is there a waiting period between deaths?"

He sighed. "I can't explain how things are here. I'm not able to do that." He was silent for a minute. "I want to give you some time to recuperate, to sleep. I think you should be able to do that if we go east. Past the lake. There are some old cabins no one uses anymore."

That didn't make any sense. "Why would people not be using the cabins?"

"Because there was a butchering there last year, and it fell out of fashion. Consequently, they're pretty safe right now. Head there. You can rest, and I'll wake you if something gets out of hand. Be careful around the others. I can't know what they're being told, ever. They could turn on each other in a hot second. X and Y, as you call them, they're brothers. One of them could be told to murder the other. It's just you and me, Eileen. Like it or not. At the end of this, it's only the two of us."

Unless he decided to have me murdered so he could get

a new human. I pushed that thought from my head. "Is it worth it, Tim? When I get out of here, is the next place worth it?"

He didn't answer, and maybe that spoke volumes.

I ran where he told me to, every muscle in my body aching, but not as much as the pain in my soul. Eventually, the cabins came into view. A slaughtering had happened here? I shuddered. "Tim, if it came to it, I don't think I could slaughter people. And if you make me... I'm not sure what would happen to me. I'm not sure I could survive it."

He spoke again for the first time since I'd started running. "You might be surprised what you can survive."

TIM DIDN'T LEAD me to a specific hut, so I just went into the first one I reached. It only had the one room, just about long enough for me to stretch out on the bare bed to my right. It didn't have a mattress. Instead, it was covered in dark blood stains. I wasn't going to sleep on that, but then, the floor wasn't much better. Someone had bled all over the wooden planks, hell, even all over the walls. This had been a bloodbath, and I bet several people died in here. No, I wasn't going to stay here. I could almost feel the ghosts of the dead waiting for nightfall, waiting to haunt me as soon as it was dark.

The next cabin was a little bigger but even bloodier. The third didn't have a bed, but the chair inside didn't have the same telltale signs as the furniture in the other huts. I doubted that there hadn't been violence in here, but at least it wasn't all covered in dried blood.

A tiny iron stove was crammed into one corner, a bucket next to it filled with logs. The people in here had probably been killed before they could even switch on the stove. What a nightmare.

It was far too warm to even think about putting on a fire, so I simply locked the door and sat on the chair, waiting for something to happen. Tim was quiet, leaving me to my own devices.

I was hungry, starving actually, but the small shelf above the stove was empty. I couldn't even remember when I'd last eaten.

"Tim?" I asked aloud.

No response. I hated how I always had to listen to him, but he wasn't always around when I needed to talk to him. He had choices. I didn't.

"I'm hungry."

Not a word. Was it safe to go outside and check the other huts for food? Tim had sounded panicked back when I'd still been with the other guys, but he'd been much calmer once we got to the cabins. I couldn't hear anything outside, not even a single bird. That had to be a good sign, right?

My growling stomach made the decision for me. I got up and unlocked the door, peeking outside. The sun was slowly descending, but I'd still have at least two hours of daylight, enough to explore and scavenge. I was good at scavenging; I'd done it all my life.

I almost expected Tim to protest when I stepped outside, but he seemed to be busy with other things. What did he even do when he wasn't controlling me? Did he have a job? A family? Did he have a girlfriend? Maybe he was having wild alien sex with her just now. I grimaced at the thought of tentacles and slimy skin. I didn't have any idea what Tim looked like, but it helped to imagine him looking very alien.

The land around the lake was flat, and the usual dust clouds hid the horizon from view. A couple of lone trees stood behind the cabin furthest from me, but that was the only bit of nature. The ground here was different from the Blastlands. There, it was at least possible to find some bugs, mosses, and plants to eat, but here, there was absolutely nothing. The only source of food would be in one of the huts, unless Tim could somehow magic something to me.

"Tim?" I tried one last time.

Oh well. Seemed I was on my own.

Then I saw the critter. I didn't know exactly what I was looking at. Some kind of squirrel-slash-rat-slash-possum kind of a thing. It crawled around and then started digging in the dirt in front of me. A bunch of insects appeared, and with his four claws, he grabbed one out and ate it. I wasn't above eating insects if that was what was called for, but my stomach really wanted something more. I swallowed.

Okay, I was going to have to kill it. I had no tools and no idea how to make any. I wouldn't have made a great example of survival if I'd been born in an earlier time. I was used to some things just existing. I ran a hand through my wet, dirty hair. My clothes stuck to me, and despite the heat, I was going to get cold soon if I didn't start a fire and eat something.

I looked at my hand. I had a lot of tech inside of me but so far, in my very limited amount of time doing this, I'd had no control over any of it. Tim had done it for me.

Could I control my own abilities, and what were they to begin with?

Maybe it was a visualization thing. I needed something to kill that animal, and could I...

My head buzzed like I was suddenly filled with

electricity, and a second later, an arrow pushed out of my wrist and straight into the creature. It dropped dead.

I couldn't move for a second. In my whole life, I'd never killed anything. Oh, I was a meat eater, but even in our limited capacity to do anything on our invaded planet, most of us would never see where our food actually came from, let alone kill it.

I swallowed. I needed to eat. I had to deal with the fact that I could shoot arrows from my hand, kill rodents, and figure out how to take care of myself. I wiped away a tear that I hoped Tim and his stupid alien friends couldn't see. I'd never been a crier. I wasn't going to start being one now. I picked up my kill.

"That was impressive." Kenny's voice caught me by surprise. "That's old tech." He walked toward me. "Oh, don't mind me, I'm stalking you. But the arrow shooting? Even those of us with basic tech have that. It's helpful when..."

He stopped talking, abruptly, staring out into space. A second later, he hit the ground convulsing wildly. I gasped, dropping the dead rodent onto the ground.

"Kenny?" I grabbed onto his shoulder. "Tim, something is wrong with Kenny."

He didn't answer me. I held onto Kenny as hard as I could. Was he having some kind of seizure? Was his alien doing this to him? I didn't know this blond guy, he was likely pretty crazy, but he was one of four people I'd met since I got into this place, and I wasn't going to lose him to some kind of seizure. Not like I'd lost my father. I gasped as the realization hit me. Yes, this was how my father had died. A seizure brought on from an unexplained infection he'd gotten after he'd cut himself at a warehouse at work. This was just how he'd died, and I'd stood there, doing nothing.

Just like I was doing nothing now, because there was never anything I could do to save anyone.

I held him tighter. "Listen to me, Kenny Whatever-your-last-name-is, you're not going to die. You're not going to die because, damn it, I say so, and whoever you are that is controlling him, you knock this shit off right now, or so help me, when I get near you, I'll shove my arrow so far up your ass, you won't shit for a week.

"Tim, if you can hear me, do something! Please!"

No reply. I was on my own. Kenny's head was bumping against a rock on the ground, so I sat down and held him in my arms, making sure he didn't hurt himself. I wish my arm was magically shooting medicine just like it had that arrow, but I guessed the aliens hadn't thought of that. Maybe Kenny's seizure was even inflicted by his controller. If that was the case... No, there was nothing I could do. Nobody I could attack. Not that I would have known how to anyway. I had self-defense skills, yes, but I didn't know where the aliens lived, what their weaknesses were, how many limbs they had.

I was stuck here with Kenny, completely helpless.

Suddenly, something glinted in the air above me. I dived to one side, but it wasn't a blade like I'd expected, but a small drone, its four propellers whirring silently. It hovered in the air in front of me, obviously wanting me to do something. I got up and walked around it until I saw the opening on one side of the drone. Kind of expecting it to attack me any second, I quickly snatched the tiny bag from the inside of the drone before stepping back as fast as I could. The drone didn't hang around but lifted up in the air and flew off, disappearing into the sunset.

I looked down at Kenny. He was still seizing and didn't seem to be getting any better. This had better be medicine.

I unwrapped the strange waxy paper that I'd taken from the drone to reveal a pack of silicone patches, the kind we used to have back when I was a child, before everything went to pieces. Medical patches that released their drug slowly and continuously. I had to trust that this was what Kenny needed.

There were no instructions, so I simply lifted his wet shirt and put one of the patches on his chest. There was nothing but hard muscle there, sculpted by the fight to survive. He was gorgeous, but that didn't matter, not when his entire body was shaking. Blood was seeping from his mouth; he'd probably bitten his tongue. Hopefully, the patch would take effect soon.

There were four more in the bag. Was I supposed to use all of them, or were they for future seizures? Could I give Kenny an overdose if I put another on him? It would be ironic if I ended up killing him with what was supposed to save him.

A strange crackling sounded in my head, painful and loud, making me close my eyes to focus on what was going on.

"Can... hear..."

Tim's words were garbled and distorted.

"Tim! I can hear you!"

I shouted the words out loud, even though I knew I probably didn't have to.

"...they... coming... run..."

"Who's coming? I've got Kenny here; I can't run. I need to fix him, I..."

"Go!"

His voice was panicked, even though I only heard half of his words. He was scared, actually scared for me, and that made me terrified. But I couldn't leave Kenny.

I opened my eyes, ignoring the pounding in my head. Blue eyes were looking back at me. Kenny was conscious, no longer seizing, and I hadn't even realized it.

He slowly licked his lips, wiping away the blood with his tongue. I wished I could offer him some water, but I didn't have any.

"How are you feeling?" I whispered.

"Been better," he rasped. "What happened?"

"I'm not sure, you collapsed and started shaking. I didn't know what to do; I couldn't stop it, but then this drone came and dropped some med patches." I pointed at his chest.

His eyes widened. "What did you give them in return?"

I frowned. "What do you mean?"

"The aliens don't give charity, never. They don't help unless we give them something in return. A promise, a deal, something that satisfies them. I've heard of people running around naked for two days because it turned their handlers on. Others have had to hurt themselves because again, the handlers get off on that."

"I didn't do anything," I muttered, trying to remember what I had said in my desperation. No, I'd definitely not said something that could be interpreted as wanting a deal. "It just arrived."

"They don't give charity," Kenny repeated. "I just hope they take their price from me, not you." He groaned as he tried to sit up. I moved to help him, but he shook me off, clearly unwilling to show any more weakness in my company. Damn him. I ignored his protests and grabbed him under the arms, helping him up until he stood on wobbly legs.

"Tim said we need to run," I explained before he could protest. "You don't look like you'll be able to, but we can hide out here in the cabin until whatever danger is over. We've even got that rodent to eat."

I smiled, trying to make light of a shitty situation.

"He told you to run? Again?"

I nodded. "But he sounded even more urgent this time."

"Then you should go. Leave me here, I'll be fine."

"No way. You can barely stand straight, you're in no fit state to be on your own."

He pushed me away, but he was too weak to move me.

Suddenly, pain rushed through my head, and I screamed, clutching my forehead as burning fire raced over my skin. If this was Tim's doing, I was so going to kill him.

"Run! They're almost there!"

His voice was loud and clear again this time, but it also hurt like hell. Every word was a dagger in my brain, twisting and pushing until there was nothing but agony.

"They will leave him alone, they only want you, so run, run now!"

I wanted to tell him how the pain wasn't going to let me run, but then he was gone, and I could see again. My head was clear, but my heart was filled with fear.

It was good and fine for Tim to give me instructions like that, but Kenny was the closest thing I had to a friend on this crazy world. I didn't know what had happened to make him seize, but I wasn't leaving him alone. Whatever he was, he was my... crazy guy I'd woken up next to in a cage.

"What is he saying to you?"

I swallowed. "Nothing." Okay, so I lied.

Kenny looked around. "The last time I was here everyone went crazed. Including me. I could only see red. When I came back to myself, most everyone was dead. Most of the people I knew anyway. Clay was still alive. X. Y. Some of the rebel mob that's always running around. It was like a... culling. I think I killed a lot of people, and I have no memory of it." He shrugged. "Not the first time. Sometimes they like to change up the players."

I shivered as we walked back inside. "Kenny, you make it seem like we're in a game."

"We are."

A boom sounded in the distance, and Kenny winced. "Speaking of the fucking rebels."

"Rebels?"

"Oh, they're the craziest of all of us. Make me look downright sane." His smile shocked me. That was smile worthy? "Come on." He took my hand. "Grab the bed. I'm too weak. Fuck me, I'm like a baby. I don't know if the rebels know about this, or if their handlers are telling them. It's worth a shot. See that hatch? Pull it up."

I did as he said, and sure enough, a compartment opened up. It was dark, but I could make out the top of the stairs. "Come on. I'm going to need you to pull the bed back over us and close the hatch. Let's hurry."

His version of hurrying was still slow, but we managed to get in, and I did get everything reset. I supposed it would just matter now about whether or not our handlers hid us. There was barely enough room for us inside. This must have been some sort of storage place. Probably made for bedding.

Footsteps over our heads made me catch my breath. Kenny looked up and then at me. We lay flat on our stomachs. He shook his head as if to tell me to be quiet. I didn't need that reminder. If these strange days were teaching me anything, it was that I did have a pretty good survival instinct, but I was also really averse to running away from things.

Kenny put his arm around my shoulders. It felt nice to

have that there. We were in this together. The footsteps passed over us again, and then the sound of a door closing met my ears. Kenny shook his head again. He didn't trust it, and since he'd been doing this longer, I was going to trust him to know. A crack of light through the floorboards illuminated the dusty spiderwebbed space where we resided.

Next to me, Kenny's eyes started to shut. He jolted and then looked at me, his voice was so low I could barely hear it. "They gave me adrenaline to wake me up. I'm crashing. I'm sorry. If you have to, leave me."

I wasn't going to do that. He didn't know I'd already denied a run order to stay with him. His eyes closed, and this time, his head fell forward. I managed to reach out and grab it so that it didn't clunk and instead, laid it down quietly on the wooden, dirty floor.

I rubbed his back. Truth was, I had no idea why he'd seized to begin with or what was going to happen. Eventually, as the room darkened, I couldn't keep my eyes open either. I closed them and slept with one ear open to the world.

◈

I DREAMED I WAS FAR, far away from the dirty storage area where I found myself and would gladly have remained in green pastures with clean sunlight and a warm beverage in my hand, but next to me, Kenny woke up. His movement roused me, and I opened my eyes, still not able to see him.

"You okay?"

He spoke to me in the darkness. "You stayed?"

"Of course. I'm ridiculously hungry but otherwise fine."

We whispered. I didn't know how long we'd been down

in the space anymore. "You okay?"

Kenny sighed. "Nothing of course about it, Brown Eyes. If my handler ordered me to kill you right now and took over my body, ordered the tech to do it, I'd have to kill you. There is no safety, and at the end of the day, it's every man or woman for him or herself."

I knew that was true. "Would you like it? Killing me?"

"No," he laughed. "Some people... when the kill order comes in... I just do it. I have to. And I hate them. Some people I try to fight it. You're in the second category."

"Thanks." I smiled. "So, we'll be each other's second category."

Kenny kissed me. In the dark, I hadn't seen it coming, but I didn't object when it happened. I'd love to lose my mind to something physical like that for a while. His tongue pushed through my lips, and I met it with my own. He tugged me closer. It was awkward. We were both on our stomachs. I didn't think we'd have enough room to roll onto our sides, so this face-to-face kissing was about as far as we were going to be able to go.

He sighed, the smallest sound, and it moved through me like a hot breeze. Just like that we stayed, his soft, warm mouth on mine, and each of us breathing into each other like we needed the other for air. Eventually, he pulled back. "Well, that's a first since I've been here."

"Kissing?"

He paused. "Well that, and also the fact that I have a raging hard on. Can't say that's happened since I stepped through the gate and woke up in the cage here. How are you here? How are you this person? How do you make me feel... human again?"

I didn't have answers for him, and that didn't seem like the kind of questions that needed answers anyway.

[5]

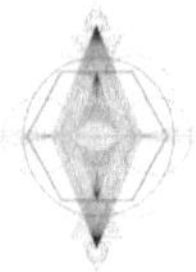

We stayed in that cramped space until neither of us could keep still any longer. My legs were cramping, aching to be moved. Tim was still quiet. When he'd spoken to me, his connection had been strangely different. Had someone tampered with it? Was he unable to talk to me now? It kind of made me scared, even though I knew he was like a parasite in my mind. Still, he'd been the only one who was able to give me directions, explain to me what the hell was going on.

Kenny insisted on going up first. His movements were faster than last night, but he still wasn't back to full strength. I'd have to ask him about his seizures, but now didn't seem like the right moment. We had to eat, move, survive.

He held out his hand like a gentleman helping a lady, helping me up the last step. He must have moved the bed. I grimaced at his outstretched offering. This wasn't a place for ladies. Manners didn't exist in this world, and rightly so. They could get you killed.

The rodent was no longer there. So much for breakfast. It should have made me scared that someone had been in the hut, just above us, while we'd been sleeping, but I was too tired to be afraid.

"What now?" I asked Kenny as soon as I was done with stretching my aching body.

"Is your handler giving you any instructions?"

I shook my head. "Not a word."

"Neither is mine. Guess that means we can do what we want. Shall I show you one of my favorite places?"

"Is there food?"

He grinned. "Maybe. If we're lucky."

"Guess there's nothing else I'd rather be doing. It's not like we have a host of options."

Kenny's grin grew wider, and a hint of craziness appeared in his eyes. "I could think of a few. Fucking you right here against the wall is one of them."

I held up a hand. "Whoa, don't get too eager. That kiss was fine, but this isn't the time or place for anything else."

His smile slipped a little. "You don't want me?"

Puppy eyes blinked at me. "I didn't say that." I sighed. "Let's just go and get out of this place. I have a bad feeling about staying."

He turned away, hiding his expression. I'd disappointed him. Well, so be it. I wasn't going to fuck a random guy who I'd only just met in a hut where he'd killed people in the past. That was entirely too creepy. Besides, I had no contraception here, and getting pregnant would be a death sentence in this environment. No, there wasn't going to be sex between us any time soon. I opened the closet and grabbed some of the clothes hanging in there, fully dressing for the first time in a while. I was glad for the clothes, and despite being pissed at him, I handed him a shirt, too.

He stepped outside, and after taking a deep breath, I followed him.

The sun was rising quickly, drawing over the dusty sky. Did the air ever clear here? Would we ever be able to see far enough to make out where we were? We'd stepped through a gate into Purgatory City, after all, but there was no city here, unless it was underground. Or maybe in space, where the aliens were. Or maybe they'd made it up completely. By now, I believed everything was possible.

"This way," Kenny said gruffly. He was walking a little unsteady, but I wasn't going to comment on it. He didn't want to seem weak, and that was fine by me.

I caught up with him and walked by his side in silence. I half-expected Tim to shout at me for not having run away, but he stayed just as quiet as Kenny.

We walked for half an hour over the hot sandy ground until my mouth was parched.

"Is there a stream somewhere?" I asked, licking my dry lips. "I'd kill for a bottle of water."

He chuckled. "Don't say that too loudly, or people might take you at your word. We've killed here for less than that."

I swallowed hard. I had to remember what kind of place I was in. One without laws and morals. Kill and be killed, that was the law of this land.

"We'll reach a little lake in five minutes or so. The water isn't the best, but it's drinkable. At least, it's never made me sick."

"Where do you get your food?"

I'd never seen him eat anything, and I'd really like some of my own.

"Sometimes my handler will tell me where to find something. They occasionally drop supplies, but by the time I get there, most of it is taken, and there's always the chance of someone murdering you over a tin of beans. There are some people who I barter with, the ones who're not completely crazy yet, although again, I only do that because I can defend myself. I wouldn't recommend you doing that. But don't worry. I'll make sure you get some food."

I stopped, staring at him. "Why?"

"Why what?"

"Why are you helping me? Why aren't you just leaving me to my own devices?"

"You stayed with me. You somehow managed to get me medicine. Don't you think that's worth something?"

No, actually, I didn't. And I was convinced there was something he wasn't telling me. Maybe his handler had ordered him to help me. Maybe there were other reasons for it. Whatever it was, I wasn't going to rely on Kenny to look after me. I wasn't some weak girl who couldn't survive on her own. I'd survived out there, in the Blastlands, and I was sure as hell going to do the same here.

We continued on in silence. There were no sounds around us. No insects flying, no birds singing. It was an eerie quiet that made me antsy.

"Fuck."

Kenny stopped in his tracks, pointing at a crusty patch of mud. "That used to be the lake."

I gaped. That had been the lake? "What happened to it?"

"I guess they're redesigning." He ran a hand through his hair. "All right. We're going to have to kill something to eat. You got that rodent. Think you could do something bigger?"

I stared at him. "You can't say something like 'they're redesigning' and expect it to just stop there. Please explain things to me. You say this is a game. Well, how do I win to get out of here?"

He smirked at me. "Brown Eyes, if I knew how to win, do you think I'd still be here?"

"Eileen." Tim was finally in my ear, and I hated that it was a relief to hear from him. "Don't do that. Don't ask questions like that. It's going to get you killed, and fuck, when I tell you to run, run. I'm trying to keep you alive."

Yes, but I still had the same questions as before. "Tim, someone has to explain it to me. Or I'm going to go mad. I"

Kenny interrupted. "It's about the tech, Eileen. It's always been about the tech." He grabbed his ear. "You'd have figured it out sooner or later anyway. And there is nothing after this except death. Stop talking to the alien, and let's go."

I shook my head. "You know what? Rather than me stopping, maybe you should start talking to yours."

"You want me to talk to my handler?" Kenny laughed. "Sure. I'll talk to him. Hey, Handler, if you can hear me, thanks for the fucking seizure while you updated my tech. I love that, you know. Yeah. It's an annoying quirk, and I still can't figure out why you guys don't put me down. Oh, maybe because I keep winning every time you try to kill me. Now, we could use some food, so we're going to go kill something."

We stood in silence until I finally had to say something. "What did he say?"

"Nothing," he shouted at me. "They don't talk to me, except to say things like kill. That is what happens here. So stop making friends with the dude who is going to make you do just the same any second now. Make no mistake, Brown Eyes. You're here to kill things."

I rubbed my arms. "You know what, Kenny? I could have if we weren't here, doing whatever this is really liked you. I'd probably have had sex with you in the other world. Now? I would just like you to stay away from me. Don't pay me back. Don't do... anything. Just stay away. Okay? You've been making it clear to me since I opened my eyes that I'm going to have to do very bad things. Okay. I'll do them." I kept saying okay. I tended to do that when I got upset. "But I'm not going to be belittled or made to feel like shit all the time. Have a nice life."

I turned my back on him and hoped he would stay right there.

"When I told you to run, I wasn't talking about other people," Tim said in my head as I walked away. "I was talking about him. He's dangerous, and you need to stay away from him. There are things happening here that make the entire game unpredictable. New factions forming, new goals. It's no longer just about your survival."

"Wait, not just my survival? Does that mean...?"

He didn't reply. Typical. But it made me think. Did my performance have some sort of implications for him? Would he be punished if I lost this game? Maybe that would make my death a little nicer. Knowing that he would suffer for it. That I wasn't going down without causing my slave master some pain. Because that was exactly what he was. I had to remember that. He wasn't on my side because he liked me or cared for my well-being. No, the only reason why he helped me was to win his stupid game.

Now that I had put some distance between me and Kenny, I looked back. He was still standing there, rooted to the ground, but he didn't seem like he was going to follow me. Good. I was going to do this without him. He was too unpredictable, and he'd said himself that he would kill me, if he was forced to. Kenny was a loose cannon, and I wasn't going to be his victim.

"Where to now?" I asked Tim.

"Head north. There's a shelter that's only just been created. If we're lucky, they left some food there."

"Created?"

"The game masters like to switch up the playing board from time to time. Remove some landscape features, add new ones. Keeps the players on their toes and makes it harder for us to keep you guys alive. I only know about the shelter because I listened to a conversation I wasn't supposed to hear. Other people are on the way there, but you're much closer, you should be able to stay there for a night before they arrive. As I said, there might be food."

In response, my stomach growled. I needed to eat something, and even more importantly, I needed water. It was getting hotter the further the sun rose in the sky, and without any kind of protection from the heat, I wasn't going to make it for much longer.

"North it is," I muttered, and turned to my left, using the sun as my compass. My father had taught me how to read the sun and the stars, and now it came in handy.

"Are you going to disappear again?" I asked Tim after walking in silence for a while.

"Not unless I have to."

"What would force you to leave?"

"Things you don't need to know about. Not much further now. Maybe another hour."

I groaned. I really hoped he was right, and that there were going to be supplies at this shelter. I could eat a wild pig, and if I didn't get food soon, I'd start going crazy.

⋄

THE SHELTER TURNED out to be an elaborate wooden house with a brand-new metal roof. It looked homey, even from the outside, as if someone was living there permanently.

"Are we alone?" I asked Tim just to make sure, before realizing that I'd said "we." As if he was here in person. I needed to control myself better.

"Yes, nobody else has made it here yet. Go and explore, I'll alert you if I spot someone approach on the screen."

"How much of what I can see can you actually see? Is it like a satellite image?"

He laughed. "Oh no, it's a lot more than that."

"Tell me."

He stayed quiet. I really hoped they hadn't put a camera in my eyes. I blinked a couple of times. No, I would have noticed that, right?

Very aware that I wasn't going to have this place to myself for long, I opened the wooden door, surprised it wasn't locked. They were making it easy for us.

Benches and a large table cut from logs were strewn around a big lounge, looking comfy in a rustic sort of way. On my right was an open plan kitchen, complete with an iron stove and several cupboards. I headed straight for them, and yes, there was food. My stomach growled, but I was already opening a jar of sausages, taking two out of the brine at once and stuffing them in my mouth. Delicious.

I ate until I was full and then considered eating more. Maybe I should stuff myself. Who knew when I'd get to eat again?

I lay on the couch, ignoring the fact that I was now thirsty. The fabric and cushions seemed stiff from nonuse, but that was better than the dirt and grime. A thought dawned on me. Was there a shower with running water? A toilet?

I found the bathroom, and to my utter delight, it

worked. I turned on the water, knowing there was a question I had to ask. I was going to bathe regardless of what he told me, but I needed to know, just the same. "Are you going to watch me in the shower?"

He sighed. "I have to." Tim cleared his throat. "I am seeing that there is a change of clothes in the linen closet. And you're still clear to bathe without anyone else coming."

I dropped my shirt and climbed into the shower, letting the water run over me. There was shampoo. Someone had stocked this place like it was a residence. I wasn't going to complain. I'd likely never see the likes of this again.

Unless the game managers felt like redesigning. How often did they do that? I dried off with a towel, leaving my hair to air dry. It really was better if I left it alone. The clothes were the one size fits all uniform everyone was in, and I put it on.

The night was quiet... scary. I hated to think of it like that, but there it was. What if Tim disappeared again, and I had no idea if someone was coming? I had to know. The trick was to keep him talking. He said Kenny was dangerous, but I'd prefer his company, even with the risk. We could have been a team. Actually, if I was being totally honest, I'd preferred Kenny, Clay, X, and Y. That had been the best scenario. Group attack.

"Tim," I said his name to test it.

"Eileen? Are you going to sleep?"

No, I probably wasn't. I wanted to know my handler. What did my puppeteer think and do? "Are you? I mean you can't be at this all day."

"I'm not."

Now that was interesting. "How does that work?"

He took a beat before answering. "I'm not going to tell you. I can't. Sorry."

His voice was human but mechanical. Kenny had said that they weren't human, they were aliens, so the likelihood was they didn't speak my language. It must be translated through some kind of machine. How did I even know Tim was the same person every time I spoke to him?

If he couldn't tell me about sleep, he wasn't going to tell me about that.

"What was your planet like? Before you took over mine? What was it like?"

He was so quiet, I thought he'd left. "I didn't take over your planet, Eileen. I promise you that."

"You particularly or your people?" I pressed the issue. I really wanted to know.

"I... my people. We didn't do this to you. Enough. I can't... they'll... never mind. No more of that."

I smiled. I'd gotten more than I'd expected. "What was your planet like?"

"Beautiful. Purple moons. Easy weather. Fertile ground. It was... perfect." He cleared his throat.

I wasn't going to get any more than that. "How many people are watching us now?"

"None that I can tell in the system. You aren't being viewed. Others, yes. Your buddy Kenny seems to have taken up talking to his handler. Poor guy doesn't know what hit him."

I smiled. Tim was downright chatty, and I was the one who had told Kenny to chat. "Do you have a girlfriend, Tim?"

He didn't respond. I kind of didn't expect him to.

"Not anymore."

His reply shook the silence between us. Wow, he wasn't just chatty today, he was positively bursting with information.

"Did you split up?"

He sighed loudly. "No. She died."

"I'm sorry," I said automatically. "How long ago was that?"

"Before I left my planet. It's the reason I signed up for this mission. There was nothing keeping me."

"Do you regret coming here?"

More silence.

"No. There are many things that I would change if I could, but there are enough positives to keep me going."

"That's good."

I wish I could say the same. There weren't many things I liked about my current situation, although now that I was clean and fed, life seemed to look a little better. Maybe Tim had been wrong about other people coming to this cabin. Maybe I could make it my home.

"I need to tell you something," Tim muttered, his voice surprisingly quiet. "I'm not supposed to, but I can't keep it from you."

"I'm listening."

"The games are going to the next phase tomorrow. Right now, it's in a sort of transition phase where the new players are getting used to the dynamics, but from tomorrow, the rules are going to change. People are going to want to see blood. It won't be safe anymore."

I snorted, amazed by his ignorance. "Are you saying it's safe just now? You're deluded, Tim. I saw two people get killed by the lake. I was almost drowned myself. I wouldn't call that safe."

"It's safe compared to what's to come. So far, the only threats have been other humans. That's going to change, but I can't tell you more than that. I'm already taking a risk warning you at all."

I was tempted to ask more questions, but the resignation in his voice made me hesitate. If he got in trouble, that would mean that he couldn't guide me anymore. He seemed genuinely interested in keeping me safe, so I shouldn't put that in jeopardy.

"Should I join the others again? Being in a team would be safer than trying to survive on my own, right?"

"Not yet. I need to find out whose side their controllers are on. If they're working against me, they could easily have their men kill you in your sleep. I'm not going to take that risk, so for now, you stay here until I tell you otherwise."

I didn't like the way he was ordering me around, but his words did make sense.

I yawned, the warm shower having made me tired and sluggish. "All right, then. I'm going to sleep."

He didn't speak until I was tucked up in the cozy bed upstairs, a double bed with lots of fluffy cushions.

"Sleep well, Eileen," he whispered almost inaudibly.

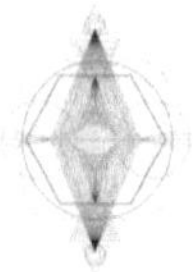

I came awake fast. I couldn't say exactly what had wakened me except a feeling of something being missing. There was the slightest noise when Tim was in my ear that was absent right then. It was like the time I'd been stuck in that storage area with Kenny. My ears were simply lacking the presence of Tim.

"Tim?" I checked just to be sure what I knew. When he didn't answer, I knew I'd been right. He wasn't there. I hadn't been able to hear the difference before, but the longer this went on, the more tuned in on nuances I was becoming. I hoped that was a good thing.

I chewed on my lips. If Tim was MIA, then I was on my own here. That very well could mean the attack that wasn't human on human was coming. I jumped out of bed, drank water, and shoved more of the sausages down my throat.

I supposed I was ready for whatever was going to come.

Or that's what I thought. I walked onto my porch—and yes, I'd started to think of it that way—and that was when I saw it. I grasped my throat. In the distance, but walking toward me surprisingly quietly for how huge it appeared, was a giant mechanical spider. My throat threatened to close up.

I was afraid of very little in this world, and truthfully, bugs didn't scare me. But arachnids were something else entirely. Spiders with their eight legs and their webs and their eating insects alive—yeah—I couldn't think about them without wanting to run and hide.

Small. Big. Hairy. Beady eyes. There was no way to make them more palatable. It was headed right for me, and I highly doubted that was some kind of accident. I bet somehow, these fuckers knew I hated spiders.

Tim had been quiet when we'd hidden in the storage area, too, and yet other times he'd been around to push off Y and help me as best he could during the near drowning. What was the deal with when he came and when he didn't?

And what did it really matter, because that spider was heading right for me.

It lifted one of its legs and shot a web right at me. I gasped, freezing in my spot. The web was going to hit me. I was suddenly shoved out of the way.

Clay lay on top of me, breathing hard. He gave me a sardonic grin. "We have to stop meeting this way."

I shook my head. "Spider."

"Robot. Just made to look and act like one. He's not a real spider. Just bolts and... fuck, I don't know robots. Just how to bring them down. Bolts and stuff. Come on."

Knowing he was right did nothing to make my unreasonable fear go away. Still, I got up. Clay elbowed me. "Hey, if I can kill it with my tech, then you certainly can. If you're going to survive in here, then you have to trust yourself and trust in your technology. That's what the handlers want to see. My guess? Yours is silent. All of ours are now. They wait and see what we can do. Are you a survivor? Or robot killer? Let's see."

He almost seemed exhilarated. Clay liked this. I steadied myself. This wasn't a person, this was a robot. I could kill a robot.

"What do I do?" I asked, starting to panic as the spider robot seemed to prepare for another attack. "Point and shoot?"

Clay nodded. "Pretty much, unless your tech is completely different from mine. It's all about the intention. Your body has to feel that you want to kill something."

I grimaced. Right now, every fiber in my body wanted to destroy that spider.

I held out my arm, the one with the alien technology inside, and hoped that this would work. The spider lifted its two front legs, steel mandibles flashing dangerously, and then it launched itself into the air.

"Kill!"

I didn't realize that I screamed the word out loud until the sound hit my ears. Luckily, it worked. A beam of light shot from between my fingers, leaving a searing pain racing through my hand. The light hit the spider straight in the eyes, and it collapsed in mid-flight.

"Well done, you're a natural." Clay grinned at me, looking completely relaxed. "Let's see what we can salvage."

I gaped at him. "You want to get close to that... thing?" I was still having a hard time convincing myself that it wasn't an actual spider.

"Of course. This is a blessing in disguise. There might be tools or weapons we can craft from it. Leaving it out here would be a waste."

"What if it wakes up?"

"It won't. That light weapon kills whatever technology

it's aimed at. I guess it fries the circuits. Something like that. Never had the chance to find out, but it's much more effective than those arrows we can fire."

He started walking toward the spider while I hung back, keeping my arm pointed at it just in case.

Clay pulled a knife out of his pocket and stabbed one of the spider's fake eyes. Nothing happened. "See, dead. Come on, I can't do this all on my own."

Gritting my teeth, I joined him, and together we pulled the spider apart, detaching its long, thin legs until the body fell to the ground.

It cracked open, revealing a hollow space filled with a black plastic bag.

"What the fuck?"

Clay seemed just as confused as me. I stood closer than him, so I pulled the bag out and opened it, revealing a heavy-duty backpack and a long, narrow parcel wrapped in cloth.

I handed the backpack to Clay and inspected the mystery object. Inside the fabric were several arrows, a separate quiver, a wooden... thing, and two flat, curved planks.

"Knowledge unlocked," a mechanical voice suddenly said in my head, making me jump. It wasn't Tim, this was a female voice that lacked any kind of personality. "Archery skill uploaded."

I waited for more, but apparently, that was all I was going to get. Weird.

I looked back at the items in my hands and suddenly, I knew exactly what they were. The wooden part was a riser, the planks were limbs, and if I attached them at the top and bottom of the riser, and put the string there, and then...

"How the heck did you know how to do that?"

Clay stared at the bow in my hand.

"No idea. There was a voice in my head, and suddenly I knew what to do. I bet I could shoot an arrow, too."

His eyes widened. "I've never heard of that happening before. Must be a new feature of this game. Go ahead, try it."

Without thinking, I put on the protective finger tab and notched an arrow. It felt familiar in my hand, as if I'd done this hundreds of times before. I turned to the house and let the arrow fly. It embedded itself right above the door in exactly the spot I'd been looking at.

Wow.

"That's amazing." Clay watched me in a mix of bewilderment and adoration. "I wish I could do that."

I stared at my hands. I'd never even held a bow before. How the fuck did I know how to shoot? Even if the aliens had somehow uploaded the knowledge into my brain, that didn't mean that my body would know what to do. Muscle memory wasn't something that could be forged. Right?

I was beginning to realize that these aliens were a lot more powerful than I thought. It was almost like magic, but magic didn't exist. It's just something we couldn't understand... yet. Maybe in a hundred years, if the world hadn't been destroyed, we would have developed similar technology.

A blush spread on my cheeks when Clay continued to look at me. I pointed at the backpack. "What's in there?"

"Food, mostly. Some water sterilization tablets, a mini stove, four emergency blankets, matches and"—he flashed me a wide grin—"a bar of chocolate."

"No way."

He pulled it from the backpack, and my mouth immediately began to water. I'd not had chocolate in a long time, ten years maybe. After the apocalypse, making chocolate wasn't a priority for mankind.

Clay removed the purple wrapper and gave me a closer look at the dark brown miracle. "Should we save this for a special occasion or eat it now?"

I didn't even need to think about it. "We might be dead in an hour. Let's have it now, or we might never get the chance."

He nodded, but didn't break the bar in half. "I wonder if we should keep a piece for the others," he said with a sigh. "It kind of feels wrong to eat it without them."

"Where are they? How did you even know how to find me?"

"It was the last thing my handler said before he went quiet. He told me where to go and to leave the others behind. I have no idea if they got similar instructions or what they're doing now. I wasn't very careful about erasing my tracks, so in theory, they might follow me here."

I supposed that made sense. "Yours went quiet, too? Let's split this five ways." My resolve at never seeing Kenny again had clearly waned. I couldn't deal with that right now. Instead, I grinned at Clay. "But maybe our pieces are just slightly bigger?"

When he grinned, he was gorgeous. The thought stopped me short. He really was. I'd been focused on Kenny and his blond hair, but Clay—those blue eyes—they could eat into my soul. I was such a sap. Always had been, but I did have a tendency to screw things up, and over the years, I'd learned how to just stay away. But now between Kenny and Clay in this strange place, I didn't know what to do with myself.

"Who's the fifth?" Clay broke me off a piece and handed it to me.

"Kenny." I sighed. "I might never see him again, but then again, if I do, it might be a peace offering."

Clay grinned. "That guy is a survivor. You'll see him again. He likes you. I mean... I get why. But he's not going anywhere. You might find a lot of people attach to you with all your new tech. That's what happened with me when I was new. I keep thinking that they'll upgrade me, but they don't. That means they're thinking of getting rid of me."

Rid of him? "Won't that mean they move you on?"

He blinked. "Eileen, people don't move on. We die. This is it for us. The whole promise of heaven? Of the better place? That's bullshit. We live in Purgatory, surviving until we die, like lab rats they can test their tech on, and... I'd better stop. They'll punish me for talking too much. But someone told me, so I'm outright telling you. Okay? This is it. And that guy in your ear... he has masters, too." He looked around. "Come on, let's go."

My whole world shattered. I stood there in the mess of the destroyed robot with my half eaten chocolate in my hand, and I tried not to fall apart into as many pieces as the technology around me. It wasn't like I didn't sort of know. I had. Things that Kenny had said. Things Tim said. Things that were just obvious. I'd have to be an idiot not to know. Yet, I'd held out hope. Why? Why did I do that?

"Eileen?" Clay put his hand on my arm. "I'm sorry. You're not okay. Are you?"

It was a terrible idea to let your enemies know what affected you. I had no experience with this. I'd never had to figure out how to relate to people who were one second my friend and the next might kill me. I wiped at my face before I turned around, giving him my back. "You go on ahead."

He didn't move. Instead, he put his hand on my arm again. "Look at me for a second."

"If you kill me can you take my tech?"

He laughed, a low sound. "And she's learning how to survive here. No. Your tech dies with you. They'd have to take me and upgrade me, but they don't seem to want to do that, as I mentioned. It behooves me to hang around you, to latch on. But that isn't why I'm asking you to turn around."

He hadn't asked so much as told me, but I wasn't in the mood to play the semantics game with him.

I turned. He wiped my tears off my face with his thumb. "Once upon a time, I had a sister and a fiancée. They're both dead. They were gone before I got here." He visibly swallowed. "I think it's been a year since I thought about them, and that... that is concerning." Clay ran a hand through his curly brown hair. "They were the toughest people I've ever known. I wasn't there the day the raiders came to steal our food, or I'd have gone down with them. I'd gone to try to get work. They must have tried to defend the place. And they were slaughtered for it. Butchered really. Possibly other things, too. I'll never know, and maybe ignorance is bliss in that case. Although speculation is hell. The point is that I haven't been responsible for making a woman cry in a very long time. I must say, I hated it then and now."

I pushed my tears down. "Sometimes I cry when I'm angry. Just because that's what happens. Drives me crazy."

"Mad tears. Yep. I'm familiar with them. Not from personal experience, but from watching them. Actually, I learned to run like hell if my sister really started to mad cry."

I laughed. How could I help myself? He was funny in this completely unamusing situation. "I'm not going to apologize for my tears to make you feel better. You don't have to feel anything about them at all. They're not your problem."

He shook his head. "I wasn't asking for an apology. I... Can I give you a hug?"

I blanched. "A hug?"

"Yes. I know. It's insane, but maybe for just one second, we could feel like human beings. And once upon a time, it wasn't such a weird thing for one human to hug another in comfort."

I swallowed, the need to mistrust warring with really wanting that hug. I let him draw me close. He was warm, steady, his heartbeat a comforting rhythm. This was it. We were here to try out tech and die. My tears welled up again. How had I been so stupid? But just for a second, I was being held by a really cute man with blue eyes who seemed to, at least momentarily, care that I was dying inside.

"You smell really good," he whispered in my ear.

So did he. "Did you find a shower, too?"

"Mhmm." He didn't expand, but I didn't need him to. All I wanted was for this hug to last forever. For the first time since I'd woken up in my cage, I felt safe. Yes, I knew that there were dangers all around us, but being in his arms made them seem less threatening. For a moment, I could let myself believe that everything would be all right. That we'd find a way out of here and live happily ever after.

"Eileen?" He sucked in his breath and tensed around me. "Don't move."

[7]

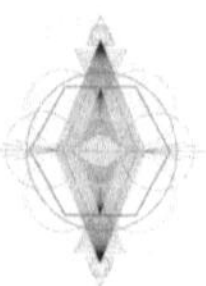

"Another spider?" I whispered, resisting the urge to turn and run.

"Worse. They respond to movement, so I need you to stay very still. On the count of three, you'll turn and throw everything you got at it. Together, we should be able to defeat it."

There was heavy doubt in his voice, which didn't exactly make me want to turn and fight whatever was approaching.

"What is it?"

"A stalker. I've only ever seen two of them, and both times, I barely managed to tell the tale. But this time, I'm not alone. You've got better tech than I did back then. Maybe you could even take it on yourself."

"But what is it?"

"A creature of nightmares," he said darkly. "Don't hesitate, just point and shoot, just like you did with the spider. Ready?"

No, not really, but he was already beginning to count.

"...two... one... turn!"

He held out his arms, and I whirled around in between them, pointing my hands at the monster.

And what a monster it was. Half metal, half flesh, with six legs, jaws that could easily bite me in half, and teeth dripping with a green substance. Poison, or just strangely colored saliva? I didn't want to find out.

Instinctively, I pushed at whatever strange powers I had implanted in my body, hoping it would be as easy as it had been with the spider. Nothing happened. I gritted my teeth and focused on the approaching stalker with everything I had. Did my light power need to recharge?

Bullets were flying from Clay's hands, hitting the monster straight in the chest, but they didn't seem to do much damage. In fact, they only infuriated the stalker, making it shake its head in anger. While it had slowly walked toward us until we'd started attacking, it now turned feral. It whined in a high-pitched screech, then pounced, launching itself into the air.

"Shoot!" I shouted at myself, following the creature's movement with my arms, hoping the light would turn on eventually. I'd never felt so out of touch with my own body. They'd turned me into a weapon but forgot to give me the instruction manual.

"Do it now!" Clay yelled, frantically shooting more bullets at the stalker.

But it was no use. The creature landed on top of me, and this time, Clay wasn't fast enough to push me aside. Sharp claws dug into my flesh, and I could almost hear my skin tear. From far away, I could hear Clay scream, but all I could focus on was the pain, the searing agony that was making it hard to think. The stalker was going to kill me. Right now, it was playing with its prey, but soon, it would kill me. Despite half of it being machine, it was easy to feel its menace rolling off it in waves. This was a monster bred to torture and kill. And I was its victim.

Tim! I shouted in my head, in far too much pain to actually say his name out loud. I'd start screaming if I opened my mouth, and I was trying to avoid that.

"Fuck. Hold on. Engaging defense system. Just a blink, it's stuck." His voice was frantic, but I couldn't have been happier to hear him. His presence gave me hope, and yes, that was completely ironic, since he was the one who'd gotten me in this situation in the first place. He and his kind.

A strange buzzing sound filled my head, and then everything went white, so bright that I would have preferred the darkness of unconsciousness. Light streamed from me, pain everywhere, screams, metal bursting, and finally, blissful silence.

◈

SOMETHING WAS BEEPING, a steady, aggravating sound that wouldn't stop, wouldn't let my brain stay in the nothingness where there wasn't any pain.

I drifted to consciousness, my gaze coming to two creatures who stood next to me. They looked at each other, not at me. Their skin was gray tinted, and their features slightly too wide, but they otherwise looked humanoid to me. Were these the aliens? What were they going to do to me? What was... How had I even gotten here?

They made strange noises when they spoke, but it banged around in my head where my tech must be translating them, and I could understand them.

"This can't keep happening," the taller of the two said, running his hand through his hair. "This is twice she's had to be fixed since we got her. They're not going to let us keep taking her back. They'll terminate the whole thing."

The shorter one drummed his fingers on the bed where I lay. He didn't look at me. "The tech jammed. I don't know why. It's like someone fucked with it. That's all I can explain. And what should I have done? Let her die? We picked her. I... I like her, and what's more, you do, too, and you don't like anyone."

He shook his head. "No more mistakes. We've done too much to get here. Yes, I like her. She's different than the others. We can fuck up. If someone sabotaged our tech, then we have to make it tamper proof." He looked down at me. "Her eyes are open. Is she seeing this?"

The second one turned toward me. "Eileen? Don't worry, sweetheart. We're going to make you so strong, no one will fuck with you ever."

I smiled at them. "You sound like Tim. You both do. Is your hair soft? It looks soft." My voice slurred, and it was like my mouth was speaking without me having very much control over it.

The taller one nodded. "We both are. But you'll never remember this, so that's okay." He turned a dial. "Have more pleasant dreams, you beautiful alien."

⚬

I woke up back in my cage. I was getting a little tired of this place. I sat up, touching my hair. "Tim?"

He didn't answer me, and something dinged around in my mind. Something I knew about Tim, but the feeling passed.

This was my first time here without Kenny. I looked around. The area was empty. Knowing I should get out of the cage didn't make me move any faster. I pushed my knees up to my head and just breathed for a second. All right, I missed the guy. I smiled. His crazy had made the dive into the deep water of the insane a little bit easier. And Clay? He'd tried to save me. Had that thing gotten him? He was worried he wasn't being upgraded. Was that the end of him?

I let out the breath I held, and I got out of the cage. There was nothing to do but go find out. I was a lab rat for tech. Fine. So help me, I'd be the last rat standing, but I wasn't going to hurt anyone I didn't have to in the process. If that meant that I died, so be it. I wouldn't forget who I was.

My bow was leaning against the cage, and I picked it up, glad they hadn't taken it away. The quiver only contained three arrows, but I was going to make them count. This time, I wouldn't rely on the alien tech inside of me. I'd rely on my archery skills, which yes, weren't really mine either. They felt more natural than all the metal inside my body, though.

I started walking in the direction where Clay and I had made our stand. At least I hoped this was the direction. My head was a little achy, and I felt groggy, as if I'd slept for a long time. Who knew, by now, Clay, Kenny, and the others could be long dead. Killed by metal spiders or that stalker thing. I couldn't decide which option was worse.

It was early morning, and the air was pleasantly cool. I was neither thirsty nor hungry, which meant they had somehow fed me while I'd been unconscious. Not that I was complaining. This meant I wouldn't have to find food right away.

I kept listening for the sounds of other people, but it was deadly quiet. Had the stalkers eaten everyone? I almost hoped they'd killed all the other humans who might turn into enemies, but then instantly chastised myself for it. I was turning into a monster. I needed to keep my humanity. My father had always made a point of keeping to his morals. "There are some lines we should never cross," he used to say. It felt easy back then, but now that I was in a place where it was kill or die, I wasn't sure if I was going to be able to hang on to those ethical lines in my mind.

After two hours, I started getting worried. I should have reached the lake by now. I'd spotted some of the landmarks on the way; I was on the right track. The lake should have been here. I'd learned that with Kenny. I recognized the lonely group of trees to my left. They'd been close to the lake, but in the other direction, which meant I should have passed it already. But there had been no water. Not even muddy ground. Just... nothingness.

A shiver ran down my back as I realized the implications I hadn't let myself dwell on enough earlier. The aliens could change the landscape. They didn't just stick to releasing lethal monsters and erecting new cabins, but they also made lakes disappear. That was beyond creepy. And they were probably watching me just now, observing my reaction. I lifted my arm and gave them the finger. Hopefully, they could see that and knew what it meant. Tim seemed pretty familiar with human customs.

With the lake gone, I didn't have any choice but to continue. I was starting to get thirsty now that the sun was beginning to burn onto the scorched landscape. I still had quite a way to go to get to the cabin. They should really have provided us with transportation. If they wanted us to fight each other, making sure we could actually meet other people would help.

A few birds passed over me, and I looked up, surprised by the sudden sight. There was almost no wildlife in Purgatory. I watched until they disappeared toward the horizon. How I wished I had wings. Fly away. Leave all this behind. Start a better life. Far, far away from aliens, spiders, and stalker robots.

After another hour of walking, I reached a forest. One that hadn't been there before. I was sure. There had been one dead tree here before; I remembered that because it had looked so depressing. Now, there were green trees as far as the eye could see. A forest should have been impossible in this inhospitable landscape, but there it was. Birches hugged fir trees, elms hid behind willows. Like someone had looked up trees in an encyclopedia and put together a random selection, unaware that they didn't all grow in the same habitat.

I slowly approached the edge of the forest, all my senses on high alert. Was this another trap?

"Hey, over here!"

X's voice made me jump. I searched the tree line but couldn't see anything besides tree trunks disappearing into shadows.

"Look up!"

A leg dangled from the branch of a tall oak tree. I walked around it, my hands gripping my bow. Just in case. His handler may have given X the instruction to kill me. I didn't know him well enough to guess whether he'd fight it or not.

"Nice to see you." He was far too cheery, sitting there on the branch, looking down at me.

I craned my neck trying to see all of him. He seemed fine, and somehow, that annoyed me. "Want to come down?"

He looked as if he was going to refuse, but then he light-footedly climbed down the tree, jumping the final bit until he was standing in front of me. He smiled at me. "You all right?"

"Mostly. Since when do you talk this much?"

"Nobody here to listen," he said cheerily, and tapped his forehead. "He's gone."

"Your alien isn't talking to you?"

"Not just that. He's gone for good. Something fried when he made me defend myself with my tech. Hurt like hell, but now I can't hear him anymore." He grinned widely. "Such a nice change."

I was jealous. Being without a constant nagging voice in your head, one who wasn't even reliable when needed, seemed like a dream come true. A few days ago, that was my reality, but now, it felt like Tim had been in my head for years.

"Do you think they're going to come and try to fix you?"

"Oh yes, they've already tried, but I escaped. Thought this forest is the perfect place to hide."

"How long has it been here?"

"I got here yesterday, so at least twenty-four hours. I hope they're going to leave it here for a while."

He sat on the leaf-covered floor and leaned against the oak's trunk. "They keep changing the landscape. Did you see the lake is gone?"

"I noticed," I said dryly. "Hard not to."

"Y has found a much better source of water though, wait until you taste it. He should be back soon, he's looking for food."

"Is he talking more now as well?"

X shook his head. "His handler is still there. I'm just lucky he hates my handler, otherwise, he would have caught me ages ago."

"You called him Y. You're brothers, right? I mean, your names can't actually be X and Y."

He grinned, showing a dimple I hadn't noticed before.

It was ridiculously cute. Dimples in a time of destruction. My thoughts were practically making me a poet. "No, but that's what everyone has called us here for so long that I can hardly remember otherwise. It's been... well, almost as long as Kenny has been here. That's how long we have. You're right. I'm Blake. He's Peter. But we do answer to X and Y. I guess I sometimes think of him that way, too."

This was a strange, strange world we lived in. He pointed up. "Safer up there. Come on. I have fruit, and it's not poisonous."

I followed him up the tree. From up there, the view was extraordinary. If I hadn't known this was man-made—or rather, alien-made—I might have gasped at how beautiful it was. Mountains. Trees. There was a lake, just much further away now—and houses? What were those about?

X handed me a piece of fruit before he straddled a tree branch. I mimicked his posture and positioned myself until I felt secure.

"It's not poisoned." He took a bite of his. "See?"

I shook my head, taking my own bite. It was sweet. "You know, I wasn't worried about you poisoning me. Without your handler, I don't know why you'd want to."

"Unless I'm lying about that in order to kill you with more stealth."

I shot him a look, and he laughed, throwing his head back. "So, this is what we call a flourishing game map. You just came from a barren one. They reset. The barren ones are when they starve us. Now, there will be plenty of food and a lot of death to go with it. We won't starve. But we will... we will still be hunted like the prey we are. It rotates. Feast. Famine. Feast. Famine."

"They just reset me, too. I guess." That was weird to think about. "Where is everyone else?"

I took another bite. This might have actually been the best fruit I'd ever eaten.

"Well, like I said, Pete is getting water. Clay hasn't been seen since you had the event with the stalker. And... Kenny? I think he's at the houses. He'd be right in the middle of that mess."

I shook my head. "What mess?"

"It becomes a little territorial when they build houses. Almost like we become factions, familial, and we go at each other like the other side killed our mother. It's a thinning. The smart people stay up here and wait."

Then I guessed I'd stay here. I lifted my bow. "I could shoot things."

His smile shocked me. There were the dimples again. "Hi, I'm Eileen. I could shoot things. You should start every interaction with that."

"If I didn't know better, I'd think you were flirting with me." I finished my fruit and threw the pit down onto the ground below.

He groaned. "Then I must not be doing it very well if you're not one hundred percent certain that's what I'm doing. I *am* flirting with you. With no alien in my head, I want to flirt with the prettiest girl I've seen in years."

My cheeks heated up. "Thanks, Blake."

"Ah... there's my real name on her tongue. Like... a song." He took my hand. "Has anyone told you the strange truth about this place?"

Maybe the fruit had made me giddy, because I really liked this. A ridiculous amount. "Something else?"

"It becomes our whole existence. Piece by piece, we forget what we were before. Until we are just this. And then... you show up, and suddenly, I'm remembering

Sunday dinners at my mother's. Even when there wasn't a lot of food, there was laughter."

It had to have been the fruit. I'd blame it on that. But I kissed him. His lips tasted sweet, like the meal we'd both shared.

In my ear, I heard a gasp, and I ignored it. For now, I was going to pretend I was also off my leash.

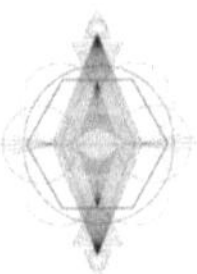

This may have been the best kiss I'd ever received. The sweetness of the fruit coupled with Blake's gentle passion... I licked my lips, craving more, but it was too late now.

Y... Peter was at the bottom of the tree, carrying two large plastic bottles, as well as a sack that also seemed to be filled with water.

He nodded at me but didn't say a word as we climbed down the tree to greet him. Blake shot me a grin, as if daring me to tell his brother about the kiss. As if. What I needed was a quiet moment to process what had just happened. And get over the fact that I was fancying not just him, but others, too. Kenny, despite his madness. Clay, wherever he may have been just now.

As if I didn't have enough worries already. Maybe that was part of the aliens' game. Put some hot men into the game so that women like me got distracted. Or maybe they'd messed with my hormones. I wouldn't have put it past them.

Peter handed us a bottle each, and I smiled at him. "Thanks."

The fruit had been full of sweet liquid, but the water was a welcome refreshment nonetheless. The air in the forest was warm and heavy, making my shirt cling to my skin.

"Find anything interesting?" Blake asked after wiping his beautiful lips.

"A hut. Not far."

Peter's voice was hoarse from misuse but melodious nonetheless. I could listen to him talk for hours, if only he didn't remain mute.

"A hut sounds a lot better than sleeping another night in a tree. Lead the way."

I liked how he didn't ask whether I was going to join them. He accepted it as fact that we were a team now. I only wished Clay and Kenny were here, too. We kept getting split up, although I bet that was the aliens' intention. Together, we were strong, and that went against their goals of making us fight and die.

"Do you think others will come and try to take the hut?" I asked Blake. "Like those houses?"

He shook his head. "I've not seen anyone enter the forest so far. With the prospect of hiding out in a well-equipped house, most of them prefer to take the risk of getting killed. They don't venture here, at least they haven't in the past. Not that this forest is the same as one we had before, but you get used to how people behave in here. They stick to their routines, while we try to change each round, confusing the other humans as well as the aliens."

"Makes sense. I'm glad we're going to have a safe spot for a while."

Peter cleared his throat. "Not safe. Monsters."

Of course, how could I have forgotten those? Humans weren't the only threats out here. I just hoped they wouldn't send another spider. I'd much prefer a stalker, or whatever else those aliens conjured up. But no spiders. Even the thought of the one I'd killed made a shiver run down my back.

"It's still going to be safer than a tree," Blake said with a reassuring smile. "And there's three of us now. We can fight whatever they send at us."

I tried to feel as confident as he seemed, but failed miserably. There was no safe place in Purgatory. We were always going to be hunted. Until the day we died, killed by other fellow humans or alien machines. How long would I be able to keep fighting? When would I get tired of it?

"Have you ever thought of giving up?" I asked quietly.

"Yes," Blake replied at the same time as his brother said, "No."

We both looked at Peter in surprise. He shrugged and kept walking, without explaining why. I would have expected it to be the other way round. Blake seemed to be more confident, but maybe that was just because Peter didn't speak. It was hard to get the measure of a man without hearing his thoughts.

We continued walking in silence. The forest grew thicker and darker, with roots protruding from the ground, making me stumble several times. The bark of the trees around us was covered in thick moss in colors ranging from white to dark emerald. Once again, I wondered how the aliens had managed to transport an obviously ancient forest to this place. Some of the trees were so tall that they had to be several decades old, maybe even centuries.

My foot caught in a root, and I tripped, ending up on all fours before either of the two men could catch me. My hands hit metal. Not soft forest floor. Metal.

"Guys..."

I swiped away the thick layer of leaves off the metal. It was old and scratched, rusty in places.

"What the fuck..."

Peter kneeled by my side and helped me clear the dirt and leaves until we could see what I'd stumbled upon. A metal square, two foot by two foot, which looked suspiciously like a trap door.

"Have you ever seen something like this before?" I asked the guys, but it was obvious from their surprised expressions that this was new for them, too.

There was no obvious handle to open it, but a slight indentation on one side might be enough to wedge something inside and force it open. Blake seemed to have the same idea, as he was already picking up a stick from the ground. I stepped aside, letting him push one end of the stick in the little gap between the hatch and the metal frame around it.

Blake groaned, his muscles bulging beneath his shirt. I'd not realized how strong he was, but after surviving in here for longer than most, it made sense that the brothers were both in good shape. I snuck a look at Peter. Yes, definitely in good shape. The way his shirt stretched across his broad chest...

The door sprung open with a click, just enough for Blake to push his fingers into the gap and pull it open. We stared into the pit. A rusty ladder would bring us down into darkness. It was too deep to see where it led.

"Wow," Blake muttered. "I've always wondered how they get the monsters into the game, since I've never seen them airdrop them with drones like they do for smaller items. And if they get monsters through this shaft from the outside world..."

"...then we might be able to escape through it," I completed his sentence.

Peter shook his head fast. "No. You might be off the grid temporarily, brother, but Eileen and I are not. We aren't escaping anywhere while we have the aliens in our ears. Trust me, they'll stop us."

"True." Blake nodded. "But maybe we can get a good look first."

He wrenched the lid the rest of the way off and without another word, jumped down. Peter shook his head fast. "He's not usually this reckless."

I didn't think I'd played a role in that, but maybe he was high on fruit and kissing, too.

"Where he goes, I go." Peter leapt down after his brother.

I stood there for a second and waited. Was Tim going to say anything? Stop me? I didn't want to be controlled but neither, did I want to be zapped.

When nothing came, I jumped down.

The guys were up a little ahead, which gave me a second to find my balance after nearly tipping over in the landing. We stood in a hallway with huge ceilings and wide walls. Everything was metal. I reached out to touch it. The room was hot, but the metal was cold. How did that work?

"You okay?" Blake walked over to me. "You look a little freaked out."

"Truth? This whole thing is freaking me out. Just when I think I've found my center, something new happens, and boom, I'm back to being freaked out."

Peter took my hand. "Come on. If we're doing this, we're doing it."

We walked together, looking all over. Every once in a

while, I'd see a vent or another cover. Air blew down on us. "This has to be transport halls."

Static blew in my ear, and I winced. Peter made a similar face. I wondered if they couldn't reach us down here. Was it actually possible to get out of here? Where would we go? Back through the gate and back to living the way we had been? Could we just walk away? With all of this tech in us?

We came to an end where the hallway entered a room. It was lit dimly, but I could make out that this was some kind of storage room. Boxes, some opened, some not, were all over the room. I couldn't discern an order. The aliens were certainly not neat.

A bang sounded, and we all darted backward behind the piles of boxes. One of them was open, and I glanced quickly down. They were syringes filled with a green liquid. It didn't look like something that should be put inside of us. I chewed on my lip. Was it poison?

Above us, the ceiling partially opened, and two flying drones holding a gurney buzzed as they flew downward. I lifted my head only enough to see that the gurney had an unconscious occupant. It took another few moments to recognize that the bleeding, beat-up resident of that bed was Kenny.

My eyes widened, and I would have rushed forward if Blake hadn't grabbed me and yanked me back.

"No," he whispered. "Too dangerous."

Only I knew it wasn't. I had to see what was wrong with Kenny, what they were doing with him, and I'd lay money on the table that my tech was better than those drones.

I was about to fight off Blake's firm grasp on my arm when the sound of more approaching drones reached me. I stilled, watching as a second gurney was slowly lowered into the room. It didn't surprise me to see Clay lying on this one. He didn't look as badly injured as Kenny, but he was unconscious and bleeding from a wound on the side of his head.

"Is this a coincidence or a trap?" Peter whispered from behind me. I was asking myself the same question. Either fate was on our side, or this was all just another game the aliens were playing with us. I was starting to think there was no luck in this world. No fate. Still... could I take the chance? If this truly was a random coincidence to have all five of us down here, then we needed to take advantage of it.

"Let's follow them," I muttered under my breath as soon as the drones were flying through a wide door into the next room.

"Are you sure?" Blake asked, but I was already on the move, running from crate to crate, staying out of sight as much as I could. I didn't know how well these drones could see, or if they were simply automated to transport the gurneys to their destination without watching for intruders.

I sensed the guys following me, but I didn't turn back. I couldn't afford to get distracted.

I stopped by the door, peeking into the other room. The drones had put down the gurneys side by side and were now hovering near the ceiling. The room seemed to be an operating room, although the blood stains on the floor made it look more like a torture chamber. My heart beat faster as I took in the tools and robots dotted around the room. I doubted Kenny and Clay would get out of here as the same people they were now. This had to be where they fitted us with new tech and repaired us when necessary. I bet I had been here, too, except that I couldn't remember.

One robot rolled toward Kenny. It looked a bit like an elephant's trunk mounted to a round column, made from metal that definitely wasn't from Earth. It shimmered and seemed to shift as the trunk robot moved. A syringe appeared at its front, pointing straight at Kenny's neck.

No, I couldn't let that happen.

I launched myself into the room before the other guys could stop me. The drones didn't react to my presence, but the robot turned toward me, the syringe now pointing at me. Fuck. I'd hoped it was programmed to heal, not to attack.

Without quite realizing what I was doing, I pulled an arrow from my quiver and notched it. Drawing the bow felt natural, like I'd done that all my life. I aimed and shot, hitting the trunk right in its front. The syringe burst, spreading green liquid all over the floor. The robot stilled for a second, and I was starting to hope that I'd killed it, but then it shook its trunk from side to side, trying to dislodge the arrow.

"Use your tech!" Blake shouted, and then both men were by my side, extending their arms. I copied them, willing my tech to come to life and destroy the robot, but nothing happened.

"Something's wrong."

"There must be something that prevents us from attacking alien tech," Peter said with gritted teeth. "The monsters are fine, we're supposed to destroy them to test our abilities, but these aren't part of that. We'll have to fight it with our hands."

That was the longest I'd ever heard him speak.

I drew another arrow. "Let me try again."

This time, I aimed at the robot's column-like body. The arrow managed to pierce the metal a little but not enough to cause any damage. Shit.

Okay, that meant fighting with my hands. Or my feet, in this case. I kicked the robot and managed to stop it from reaching me as it rolled backward a bit. My leg hurt. Tech or no tech, I wasn't meant to be kicking robots. It was like beating up the fridge in my old apartment, even though the thing never worked, it had been huge. Man versus metal, metal won. Still, I kicked again.

"Grab them. Don't let them inject them with anything. We don't know if it's helpful or poison."

My gut told me poison. I had the sense that when I'd been healed, it hadn't been by robots. I didn't know why I knew that. I grabbed the arrow from the pack I had, and rather than loading it up to shoot the robot, I jammed it straight into what had to be the eye. The robot abruptly stopped moving, smoke coming from its circuits.

Hopefully, Blake and Peter had done what I asked because right then, all I had time for was running back before that thing exploded. I hit the ground just as an ear shattering bang sounded.

"Damn," Blake grabbed me, hauling me to my feet. "That was pretty badass."

Badass? Had I heard that right? My ears kind of rang, and it was hard to tell. "Uh. Thanks."

Both of my unconscious friends—and in this situation, that is what they were—were wheeled to the side. I pulled myself up. I was going to be so frickin' sore tomorrow. I limped toward Clay and Kenny.

Peter looked over at me. "You are the most beautiful, crazy woman I've ever seen."

I blinked. "Is that a compliment?"

He pulled me to him, and before I could form a thought, his lips met mine. I startled but quickly kissed him back. There were a million things I should have been thinking about—a robot exploded, we were in a shit ton of trouble, Kenny and Clay were in big trouble, he'd once choked me under orders of his handler to see my tech, and I'd kissed his brother. But all I could think right then was that Peter's kiss could bring me to my knees.

The moment seemed to last forever and also to be over too quickly. His lips were firm but soft, and he drew me to him by the back of my neck with an ease that told me he'd done this before. I sighed against him just as he backed off.

He winked at me. "You're a crazy person, and I fucking love it."

Blake walked over and reality slammed into me. I'd been making out with him in the tree, and Peter had just grabbed me. Were they going to be okay with this, or...

His lips met mine, and I was so startled, I didn't move until I molded against him, kissing him back. He let go to smile down at me. "I should tell you that Peter and I almost always shared the same girlfriends. It's not a necessity, and if you're not into it, that's fine, too. I should just tell you that I'm not at all surprised he kissed you. We always end up attracted to the same women, and you are incredibly hot, and he's right, also a little bit crazy."

I wasn't quite sure what to say to that. I'd always been focused on survival, especially after my parents had died. There'd been no time for boyfriends, and now there were two men insinuating that they might want to be with me? That was crazy. This was neither the time nor place for it, but my heart was telling a different story, beating fast as I thought of our kiss and how I wanted to kiss them again.

A groan made me swirl around. Clay was staring at me, his eyes wide.

"What the fuck happened?"

We'd dragged the two men out of that room, away from the broken robot and the drones. Clay was propped up against a large metal storage container while Kenny was unconscious on the floor. I gently lifted his head and pushed Peter's bag of water underneath, which had somehow survived the fight. Not the perfect pillow, but it would have to do.

"I woke up at the cabin, and you were gone," Clay said slowly, his voice hoarse with pain. "I was injured, but not as bad as I am now. I walked around. Shouted. Searched for you. But you weren't there. I found some paper in the house and wrote a message, telling you that I'd be headed for the cages. If they'd taken you out of the game and given you new tech, that's where you'd wake up."

He groaned. "I never made it there. Another reaper got me close to where the lake used to be. On my own and wounded, I didn't stand a chance. Just when it had its maws open, ready to crack my skull open, Kenny appeared out of nowhere. He somehow managed to get a knife stuck in the reaper's back, and that fucker must have a semblance of a spinal cord. It went down, legs no longer moving, but I was buried underneath it. Kenny wasn't strong enough to lift it off me. I was telling him to leave me when those drones appeared. They shot us without warning. Too fast to fight them. And then I was here."

He turned to look at Kenny. "How bad is it?"

Blake had been checking Kenny over.

"I'm not quite sure. There are a lot of injuries, not all of them bad, but together, they might be a problem. He's lost quite a bit of blood. Maybe that's why the poison made him unconscious for longer than Clay."

Blake held up a small dart, about as long as my pinkie finger.

"Some kind of sleeping poison?" I asked.

"Probably. I don't think it was meant to kill. That wouldn't make sense, the reaper could have achieved that. They could have sent more monsters rather than drones. No, they wanted them unconscious to do something to them in here."

"Where is here?" Clay asked, rubbing the back of his neck. "How did you even find us?"

"Underneath the forest," I explained. "Yes, there's a forest now. We found a sort of trapdoor that led us down here. It was a coincidence that we saw the drones bringing you in."

"Our comms don't work here, so we're safe from our handlers for now," Blake added. "Although mine stopped working up on the surface. I think the aliens are having some problems with their tech."

"Thank goodness." Clay smiled weakly. "I'm going to enjoy the silence in my head. No one to tell me what to do. Paradise."

"Do you believe in paradise?" Peter suddenly asked. He

shrugged when he saw our surprised looks. "They promised us Paradise once we got through Purgatory City. But it was all a lie. There's not even a city, just this fucking wasteland. Do you think there's anything beyond here?"

Once again, he'd said a lot more words than I was used to hearing from him. I liked it. His voice was a little rough, but it fit him.

"I doubt it." Blake left Kenny's side and sat down next to his brother. "It was all just a ruse to get us here. I've never heard of anyone leaving this place unless they die. There's nothing waiting for us but death. Maybe that's why they call those metal creatures reapers. The Grim Reaper, helping us to the other side." He laughed, but there was no humor in his eyes, only sadness. "I hate feeling so powerless."

These were all the same thoughts I'd been having myself. "I guess the question is what the right thing to do would have been. Stay where we were and just... die? I was going to starve to death. There wasn't any water. Maybe I could have been trampled to death by a mob, or raped and murdered. Then I come here and, believe it or not, I've eaten more in the last days than I have in who knows how long... and I get loaded up with tech I could have to use to kill my new friends."

My cheeks heated up as I realized what I'd said. Maybe they didn't think of me as friends.

Peter nodded. "I hurt you. I... I'm not sure how to really say sorry for that."

I patted his arm. "Let's leave it alone. In all the ways I've been hurt since I've been here, you showing me how to use my tech was the least of it."

Clay looked between us. "I've never felt more like my old self than I do right now. I mean, since I got here, I've been this other person. I've had to be. But, Eileen, you make me feel like I used to feel. Almost... human."

Kenny groaned, and I got to my feet to walk over to him. I rubbed his hair off his forehead. "Hey there. Can you hear me?"

His eyes were swollen shut from the beating he'd obviously taken. He cracked them open and groaned again. "Eileen?"

"Yep." I smoothed his hair off again. It was a natural movement. I used to love to be touched, to be patted when I didn't feel well. I hoped it wasn't annoying him. "You're pretty hurt, but I think your tech is healing you, and we only need a little bit longer for that to happen."

He nodded. "You okay?"

"Am I okay?" I smiled at him. "Yes, I'm fine. You're hurt. Do you understand?"

His mind really wasn't on what I said to him. "Clay okay?"

"He's fine, yes. You helped save him."

He nodded again and closed his eyes. His breathing evened back out, but I sat there, not moving, except to stroke his hair off his forehead. He was a little bit crazy, but then again, the guys said I was, too. I leaned over and kissed his forehead where I'd stroked it.

Turning around, all three of my companions openly stared at me. I swallowed. What were they thinking? Had I done something wrong? "I think he's starting to heal."

Clay touched the ground next to him. "Come sit."

I walked over and sat down where he'd indicated. I'd somehow made things uncomfortable, and I certainly hadn't meant to. "So, um, should we stay here until we absolutely have to leave it? Explore around as soon as Kenny's on his feet, and only go back up when we are completely starved?"

Blake grinned. "Sounds good, and I have an idea. Hold on." He darted toward the boxes. "I'm going to make us some cards."

He tore into the boxes, and I sat up straighter. "How are you going to mark them up?"

"With my knife."

"Deal me in," Kenny rose from where he'd been knocked out. He didn't look better, but he was awake and apparently, intending to play this game. He limped over to us and didn't so much as sit down next to me as he stumbled onto the floor. He gave me a sheepish grin while we all waited for Blake to come back with the cards he made.

Of all the things I ever imagined doing in my life, playing cards in an underground lab with dead robots in the room next door was not one of them. Still, it felt right. Spending time with the guys without running for our lives. This was a moment of peace, and no way was I going to pass on it. We'd earned us this break. We deserved it.

Kenny was pale but smiled bravely, even though he was losing the game. Peter turned out to be the master of the poker face, only exposing his winning hand at the last moment without any of us being the wiser. I lost a few rounds, won one, but I didn't really care about winning. We laughed, we smiled, we had fun.

"Did you play a lot of games before you came here?" I asked Peter when he won yet another match.

His brother answered for him. "All the time. It was our way to escape reality. Sit in our rooms for hours, playing cards or a board game. Our parents never had much money, so cards were a cheap way of entertainment."

"It must be nice to have a brother," Kenny said quietly.

"No siblings?"

He shook his head. "I'm an only child. And an orphan. Never knew my parents. Grew up with foster parents, but when everything went to shit, they looked after themselves first. I didn't matter to them anymore. As soon as I turned eighteen, I came here. I had nothing to lose. "

I reached out and squeezed his hand. "You're not alone anymore."

He gave me a small smile. "I'm glad I survived long enough to meet you. Some days, it seemed easier to end it all. Just let the monsters kill me. Or the other humans. But I fought on, somehow knowing that something better would happen. Now I know it was worth it." He rubbed his eyes. "Although I may be lying to you. I change my background whenever it suits me. Just to let you know. I can't remember my background all that clearly. I'm easily confused."

My eyes teared up at his words. He seemed so happy, even though there was nothing much to be happy about and he couldn't remember where he came from. He was injured, we were in a place full of things that wanted to kill us, and while we had a momentary reprieve from our handlers by hiding out down here, we wouldn't be able to stay forever. We'd need food at some point.

Clay took my other hand, settling it in his lap. "He's right. I mean, I don't know his background. But the rest of what he said. It was worth waiting."

His eyes captured mine, and I couldn't look away. There was so much emotion in his gaze, but I couldn't quite figure out what he was trying to tell me.

"I don't understand," I said softly, almost a whisper.

"It was worth waiting," he repeated. "For you. You've brought us together. Given us something to fight for. We're stronger together, and now we have hope."

I scoffed. "Hope for what? There's no way out of here."

"Who knows? There might be. But right now, I wouldn't want to be anywhere else in the world."

He pulled me toward him, forcing me to let go of Kenny's hand. Clay cupped my face with his free hand, and then his lips were on mine.

I should object, or stop him, except that I didn't want to. They were all kissing me like it was the most normal thing to do. Clay's lips were strong; he was assertive, demanding. Inside of me, heat pooled in my core. My breasts tingled and then ached. These were all new feelings for me. If we'd been alone, I might have crawled up his body and begged for more. As it was, I had to force myself to stop before I embarrassed myself in front of everyone. All of this attention was going to my head. Or maybe my insides. I was hotter and needier than I could ever remember being before.

Clay's gaze was heated, and he breathed hard. He smoothed his thumb over my bottom lip. "You shouldn't be so beautiful in this crazy place. I swear, you just get prettier and prettier."

"Hey dude," Blake threw a card at him. "We're playing and, for the record, I kissed her earlier. So did Peter."

Clay smirked, his gaze not leaving mine. "I don't care. Kiss her all you want. It isn't going to stop me from doing it. I promise you that. I used to play by the rules. I did everything out there on the other side of the gate that I was supposed to, and everyone I loved died. In here, we can't own each other. The aliens already do. All we get are moments."

"Just wanted to make sure you understood we like her, too. And I think she likes us."

Kenny cleared his throat. "I kissed her first. Before all of you."

My cheeks were so hot, I had to be beet red. When I would have climbed off his lap, Clay squeezed my waist. "So, I guess we're all going to want to keep kissing you, Eileen. You woke something up in us that I thought, for me, was long gone."

"Really?" There was a smirk in Peter's voice. "I knew that mine still worked."

Clay rolled his eyes. "I wasn't talking about *that*."

I laughed. I couldn't help it. Soon everyone else was, too. I climbed off Clay's lap, and even though I was thoroughly embarrassed and somewhat shocked that I'd been publicly making out with any of them, I was also the happiest I could ever remember being.

"This moment?" I threw my cards down. I couldn't even recall whose turn it was after that exchange. "This is what happiness feels like. I'd forgotten it."

They must turn the heating system down at night in this place, because it had gotten colder since we'd arrived. Next to me, Kenny shivered. The tech was still healing him, and he'd lost a lot of blood trying to save Clay. I'd been on top of him, but he was also still healing from injury. I met Blake's gaze across the circle.

He nodded at me before he rose. "I'm going to see if there are blankets in the blown up infirmary."

Peter scooted closer to Clay. He elbowed his friend gently. "You should lie down. I don't think Eileen would think less of you for doing so."

Clay rolled his eyes. "I never sleep. Not much, anyway."

Blake came back in, holding blankets and pillows. They were slightly singed, but he passed them out.

"How is it in there?" I asked Blake.

"Dirty." He smiled at me, handing me a blanket before he gave them to everyone else. Then he passed out the pillows. I took Kenny's blanket and wrapped him in it. How was he even awake?

He scooted down onto the pillow. With wounded eyes, he smiled at me.

"This right now?" He mimicked what I said earlier. "This is who we would all be if they weren't in our ears, controlling us. Who we were when we were just us, before I lost it."

I put my hands in his hair. I'd been so upset with him, but I could hardly remember why. "My handler is okay. I call him Tim. I think he means well, but he'd hate this. He doesn't like me to be around people."

Clay widened his eyes. "You gave him a name?"

"Oh, she talks to him and everything." Kenny sighed. "Got me talking to mine. He talks to me now, too. It's weird. But she's right. They are more helpful when you address them."

Blake shook his head, lying down. "Mine is an asshole. I don't want to talk."

Peter stretched out. It looked like we were all getting ready to bunk down for the night. "Maybe he likes you. Like he wants to keep you all to himself."

"Why would he like me?" I shrugged, putting my head on the pillow.

"Because you're beautiful. And there's something about you that calls to others." Peter rose and scooted with his blanket until he was by my head. Blake did, too. At this point, it was like they were in a circle and I was the center.

Kenny smiled. "Even the aliens are taken with you, Eileen."

I rolled my eyes. That was just ridiculous. I wasn't sure

why these guys wanted me around the way they did, and I wasn't going to believe Tim had any feelings at all where I was concerned, other than wanting the tech to work.

It was so quiet after that, I could hear the air conditioning buzzing loudly. Banging from above us, things that must be moving in the area where we were supposed to be. The light was the same. It wasn't dark, but I was tired. I should have been able to sleep anyway. Still, I was up. I looked over at the others. They were all awake.

I wasn't the only one who was going to struggle tonight.

Finally, Kenny scooted forward. "Roll over, face Clay."

I scrunched up my face but didn't argue. Kenny put his arm around my waist. "Tell me a story, Eileen."

Clay scooted forward now that I faced him and put his hand on my hip. "Yes, tell us a story."

From where he was near my head, Peter rolled toward me. Blake squeezed my foot.

"I don't really tell stories. But I guess I could come up with something."

Kenny kissed the back of my neck. "I'd like to just hear the sound of your voice."

I tried to think of what to say. "My parents were really nice people. It was always bad out there, but before it got worse, my father used to take me for walks on Sundays. He'd talk to me about everything. The trees. The buildings. The birds in the sky. And it wasn't until a lot later that I realized that when he didn't know the answer to a question I'd have, he'd make it up. So for the longest time, I really did believe that the blue bird that used to fly overhead was called a blue wobble. Yep. I thought that was real. And I'd share things with people like, oh yeah, that's a blue wobble. I could never understand why people stared. Then, one day, finally someone told me. But I guess there are parts of me that still like the things he made up."

Clay smiled at me. "I like that. He just wanted to give you answers."

He was the only one to answer. I looked around. The others all had their eyes closed. I couldn't see Kenny, but his breathing was even. I hadn't talked long. They must have really just wanted to hear me speak.

Clay scooted even closer, pressing our foreheads together. When he spoke, it was a whisper. "I loved kissing you."

I nodded. "Me, too."

He kissed my mouth lightly. "Go to sleep. We're as safe as we're ever going to be right now. I'm going to try to, too."

We were so close, we practically breathed the same air. I did as he said. After a few minutes, I lifted my lids. Clay was asleep. I was in the middle of all of them, and if they could rest, I supposed I could, too.

I closed my eyes. This time, I let sleep in.

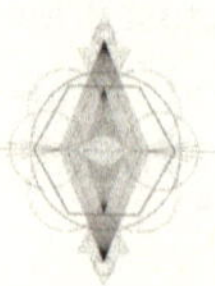

10

I woke up slowly, gently, like resurfacing from a relaxing dive in a pool. I'd not had this feeling in months. Heck, years maybe. I'd always been woken up by either my own fear or an actual threat. No nightmares this time. No monsters, real or imagined, trying to kill me. Just peaceful sleep that left me relaxed and rejuvenated. I hadn't felt this good since I'd entered Purgatory.

"You look beautiful when you sleep," Clay whispered from my right.

I slowly opened my eyes, taking in the scene. We were huddled together, limbs across limbs, our bodies entangled in a giant knot. I was facing Clay, but there was a head on my belly and hips brushing against mine. One of the guys was using me as a pillow, just like my own head was on someone's chest. It was hard to feel where I ended and the others began.

"Sleep well?" he asked, his eyes fixed on me.

"Very. How long have you been watching me?"

He grinned. "A while. As I said, you're a pretty sight when you're asleep."

"And not when I'm awake?" I couldn't help but tease him.

"You're less innocent but just as beautiful. Want me to prove it?"

"Stop seducing her." Blake groaned from where he lay. His breath was warm as he shifted around to breathe against my neck with his body pressed against mine. He must have ousted Kenny at some point during the night. "Give us a chance to wake up so that we can all have the chance."

"The early bird catches the worm. You're just annoyed I managed to snatch the best position during the night."

Blake scoffed. "The best position? Not quite."

He shifted a little, and I could no longer ignore his hardness pressing against my back. I'd heard some men woke with a hard on in the morning, but was that because he was touching me or just a random thing that happened to him every day? I certainly hoped it was me having this effect on him. It made me feel powerful, beautiful.

"Depends on what you prefer," Clay muttered, giving me a wink. "I get to see her gorgeous eyes and kiss the lips that are parting for me. If only you could see the way she's looking at me right now. Pupils dilated, cheeks flushed, her mouth slightly open, ready to be kissed..."

I laughed. "You're lying."

"Am I? Are you sure?"

I pressed a hand against my cheek. All right, my skin really was warm. Maybe I was blushing, so what. I was surrounded by four men who had all told me last night that they wanted me. I was allowed to be a little turned on by that.

I met Clay's teasing eyes. "Kiss me, then."

"I thought you'd never ask." The last word disappeared

into his kiss as his lips descended upon mine. He was gentle and slow, not the claiming kisses of the night before, but no less intense. A small moan escaped me as I opened my lips, letting him in. His tongue swiped across my bottom lip then met my own, and the dance began.

Blake wrapped his arms around my waist and pulled me closer against him, against his erection. Oh my. What a way to start the day.

"I'm not sure how I got usurped from where I was," Kenny's voice spoke from my stomach, where he'd made me his pillow, "but I'm not complaining either."

My shirt must have ridden up, and he kissed the exposed skin right there. I gasped against Clay's mouth, and he smiled. Next to me, Blake started to kiss my neck. This was really happening? Three of them... No, wait, four. I was lying partially on top of Peter. His hand scooted down my pant leg and found the spot right over my underwear.

His voice was low when he spoke. "Guys, she wants this. So wet, I can feel it through her panties."

I did. I arched my back, which took my mouth temporarily from Clay. I didn't know anymore which one of them was which body. They all felt male and oh so hard.

There was something I had to say, and I needed to get the words out before Peter slipped his fingers inside of my undies and went where I wanted him to go. But how could I think when Kenny pinched my nipple?

"Guys." I panted more than spoke. "I need you to know that I have no idea whatsoever what I'm doing. I wish I did. But if I do something... you know... wrong..."

Clay shook his head. "Wrong isn't possible in these circumstances. But if you want to slow down, we can..."

A bang sounded. It was close. Like someone had

opened and closed the path to the ceiling. Clay's eyes were huge. "Fuck."

Everyone moved fast, even Kenny, who must have been feeling much better. We had to hide, and we had to do it immediately.

We scattered, using the crates and containers in the room as hiding places. I ended up crouched between two metal boxes with Kenny.

"You okay?" I whispered.

"Feeling much better. My tech must have healed me overnight. Almost back to normal."

Good, that meant he would be able to run if we had to. Maybe we should have left this place rather than camp out here overnight, but what would the alternative have been? Back into the forest where reapers and metal spiders may have been lurking? We were in danger no matter where we were hiding.

A strange whizzing noise sounded from behind the door leading to the tunnels. We'd closed that door last night, and I was glad Peter had been aware enough to push a large crate in front of it. At the time, I'd been worried he was locking us in, but now I was grateful for that additional protection between us and whatever was trying to get through.

Another door led to the operating room, but that room had no other entrances or exits, so we were safe from that side. If necessary, we might be able to retreat to that room, although there were more hiding places in this one. Trouble was, I hadn't considered the hole in the ceiling through which the drones had entered yesterday. It was covered by steel right now, but it could open at any moment. If they couldn't get in through the blocked door, they'd have an alternate way. We wouldn't be able to use the hatch to get out though. It was too far up, and there wasn't a ladder anywhere in the room. Nor did we have a key to open it. Fuck. We were trapped.

Kenny put a hand on my shoulder, and I almost jumped.

"Sorry," he muttered. "You're breathing too fast. Calm down."

"We're trapped," I hissed under my breath. "That's not exactly relaxing."

"Maybe it's just some drones who'll give up soon when they can't get in. Once they're gone, we can get out of here and explore the tunnels some more."

His words were echoed by a loud bang. A dent had appeared in the metal door.

I balled my hands into fists. "I don't think they're about to give up."

A noise to my left made me whirl around. Clay had left his hiding spot and was running into the lab. I didn't dare shout to ask him what the hell he was playing at. He probably had some kind of reason. Maybe we should all relocate there and take our last stand in the operating room. There had to be some scalpels there that we could use as weapons.

Another bang, another dent. They were trying to break through. So far, the door in the ceiling stayed shut, but for how much longer?

"Shall we?" Kenny whispered, apparently having the same thought I'd had.

I nodded. "One door to guard is better than two."

I took a deep breath and got to my feet. Kenny followed me as I ran into the other room. Peter and Blake were close behind. I turned to close the door behind them, then cursed.

It was a sliding door, not one with a handle that we could bar from the inside. Fuck. Fuck. Fuck.

"I've found a way out!"

Clay was grinning at us from the other side of the room, pointing at a vent in the wall. He'd removed the cover, revealing a narrow passage. I was going to fit in there, but would the guys? It seemed far too small for them, but maybe I was mistaken. I really hoped so. This could be our only way we might survive this.

"I have no idea where it leads, but it's better than staying in here, right?" He was still smiling, despite the tension in the air. The knocking against the door was increasing, and I didn't think it would withstand the assault for much longer.

"Will you fit?" I asked. "It's pretty narrow."

Clay shrugged. "We'll just have to make ourselves real small. Not breathe. Roll in our shoulders. Somehow, we'll manage. You go first though, you can scout ahead while we squeeze ourselves into there."

This was not the right moment to remind myself that I didn't like enclosed spaces. Not at all. We had to hurry, there was no time to stay and think of alternatives.

I gripped my bow and climbed into the vent. It was just about high enough for me to move on all fours, but the guys would have to wiggle along on their bellies.

I moved as fast as I could. All five of us had to get through this, and I wasn't going to let anyone die because I was a slowpoke.

Clay had called this the way out, but after ten minutes of crawling and not really having any idea where I was, I wasn't sure if it wasn't the vent tunnel to nowhere. I thought Peter was right behind me, but I couldn't turn my head to look, due to the tightness. All of us were being pretty silent. Only the occasional grunt or oomph caught my ear.

Finally, a vent appeared above my head. I chewed on my lip. That would likely take us back into the fighting we'd been hiding from. I sighed. There really wasn't any choice. We had to get out of here eventually. Or else we'd starve to death.

With little choice but to continue on this endless trek or go upward, I picked upward. I banged on the vent, which came off easily, and hoisted myself up. I stayed on my stomach, thinking that remaining low was the best thing to do.

I didn't know exactly where I was, not that I expected to. They'd changed the landscape. Still, I looked up, and we were closer to the houses than I'd expected to be.

Peter came up next, groaning as he stretched his arms over his head. "That was tight. You okay?"

I never got to answer him while Tim returned, shouting in my ear. "Where the hell have you been?"

I winced. "Taking a breather."

"Do you have any idea how worried we've been over you? The shit you've caused?"

Wow, he'd cursed. I wasn't sure if I'd heard that before. "We?"

He was silent for a second. "Never mind that. Where did you go? What did you do?"

It was interesting that he didn't know. I'd have thought they'd have informed him about the problems they'd had down below, but maybe not.

Peter fell over, grabbing his head. Were they punishing him for vanishing?

Kenny was up next. One by one the guys emerged, each one of them taking a physical lashing for what we'd done. Even Blake's alien seemed to be back online.

Peter raised his gaze and met mine. He placed his hand

over his mouth, and I understood what that meant. He couldn't talk, again. I looked at Blake and saw a similar reaction. My heart clenched. I'd loved hearing them speak. They were back to being silenced. X and Y. The aliens' perfect killers.

"Eileen, step away from them."

I didn't move. Tim could piss off. I was not going to leave my friends. He may think that these men were just my random companions, but in fact, they were so much more than that. I wasn't going to tell him that though. I had a feeling he wouldn't like it.

Suddenly, Kenny screamed, his hands on his ears, his knees buckling. I ran to his side while shouting at Tim. "What's happening?"

"You need to leave, now. They're being punished, and this is going to get ugly. They might be forced to kill each other, and I don't want you anywhere near them when that happens."

Kenny's scream turned into a choked sob. His eyes were closed, and he didn't react to me shaking his shoulder. He was shaking all over, and his teeth started grinding as if he was in pain. It hurt like hell, seeing him like that.

"I'm going nowhere," I snapped at Tim. "Is there anything you can do to stop that from happening?"

"Is there..." He sounded incredulous. Silence followed.

X started screaming at the same time as Y. Clay was staring at them, frozen, his eyes the only part of him that was moving. What were those aliens doing to them?

"Please, Tim," I begged, hating myself for it. "I need them to survive. You want me to survive, right? Well, they're going to help me. I can't make it without them, and you know that. You can't be here with me, so they will have to in your stead."

"If I could, I would." His voice was strangled, full of emotion, despite the mechanic undertones of it.

"I know that. Now, help them, please?"

"It's not us doing that to them, it's their handlers. But at least one of them owes me. I might be able to come to an arrangement. But while I do that, you need to move away from them. A safe distance, in case they're given the kill order. Otherwise, I won't try and help."

Everything in me was fighting to stay close to the guys, but my rational mind won. I had to follow Tim's instructions if I wanted him to stay on my side. He was the most powerful ally available, and I'd be stupid not to make use of that. Besides, he actually seemed to care for my well-being.

I walked away until I reached a solitary oak tree that definitely hadn't been there before. Its bark was thick with age, its leaves more colorful than they should have been. This tree wasn't quite natural. Not artificial either, but something had happened to it that made it more intense somehow. I clenched my fists and watched from afar as the guys were hunched over in pain. I felt guilty for not sharing their suffering. Watching was almost worse than being in pain myself.

Crackling static filled my head, and I jumped in shock. "Tim, is that you?"

A strange whizzing noise followed the static, making my teeth hurt. "I've managed to talk to Clay's handler. He's willing to make a deal. But you have bigger problems. There's a group of other humans headed your way. They're ordered to kill whoever they meet, and there's no way I can persuade their handlers to change those orders. You'll have to run."

"But what about the others?"

"I can't help them," Tim shouted, real panic in his voice. "If you don't leave now, you're dead. Please, Eileen, trust me. As soon as you're safe, I'm going to warn your companions' handlers of the approaching danger. Now run. Just run."

"Eileen!" Clay shouted from afar, waving at me. He didn't seem to be in pain any longer. Thank goodness.

I sprinted toward him and leapt into his arms. He held me tight, drawing me so close that there was nothing left to separate us.

"We need to go," he whispered gently, his breath kissing the nape of my neck. "My handler has warned me. They're coming for us."

I nodded. "I know. Mine, too. Apparently, yours owed mine something. Weird to think of them bartering with us. But we can't leave them."

Clay looked over his shoulder. "But what can we do?"

I pointed at the trees. "We go up, and when they get close, we blast them."

Clay looked up. "All right."

He bent down and put his hands together. I stepped on the linked fingers, and he hoisted me up onto the tree branch. I straddled the branch and then leaned down to give him my hand. He took my offering, and I helped pull him up.

We nodded at each other like this was the most normal thing in the world.

Kenny, X, and Y all rolled on the ground. I swallowed. "This is awful."

"The worst." Clay shook his head. "We've got to figure out how to fix this."

I had some thoughts on that. "We have to make it worthwhile to them to keep us all together and not hurt them." I chewed on my lip. "Let's keep them alive, and then we'll propose a deal."

He gaped at me. "To our handlers?"

Yep. We had things they wanted. If we got through this, I was going to suggest he let us put on a show. If this was about the tech, then so help me, we could show the tech. We could win. Together.

I shook my head. First things first. The crowd coming to kill us arrived in the distance.

"You're serious with this?" Tim sounded different. The rhythms of his mechanical voice were flatter. I wasn't even sure how that could be, but it was.

"I am, Tim. I'm not running. You trust your tech, right? You put it in me."

He sighed. "It'll hold. We... I don't want this for you." Sometimes he screwed up his pronouns. Must be an alien thing. "But go ahead, Eileen."

"Hey," one of the crowd shouted. "There they are. Get them!"

They charged. I fired.

For once, the tech did what I wanted. I blasted the ground in front of them as they approached, throwing them backward.

"What the fuck?" Someone shouted.

The others' handlers must have clued in to the fact that we were under attack. Y lifted his head. He looked battered, staggering. None of them were going to be in any position to fight.

Clay winked at me. "You're so hot when you're blasting. But then again, you're always hot."

"Is he fucking for real?" Tim made a gagging noise. "You *can't* like that."

I winked back at Clay, but spoke to Tim. "I do, actually.

I like all of them. If you want to be technical, I've hooked up with all of them. But we're fighting. Maybe we can talk romance later."

I blasted again, ducking as someone fired back at me. This time, a mechanical screech sounded in my ear. Laser shooters pushed out of my hands. I shot forward, a red glow exploding around the man I blew up. Clay fired next to me. Together, we moved like we'd been made to do so. Maybe we had.

The first enemy reached Kenny, who was barely able to keep upright. I hoped his handler was regretting torturing his charge now. I pointed both arms at the man, and power burst from them, hitting the attacker right in the chest. He froze, shook, collapsed. One less to worry about. More and more came running, but Clay and I had the perfect strategic position. From afar, we were hidden in the foliage, and while they tried to shoot at us, none of them actually managed to hit us.

"I didn't know there were that many people living in Purgatory," I panted in between blasts.

"There are more. A lot of them stay on their own, hide away in the hope they'll survive that way. I don't know how that works with their handlers. Mine would never allow that." Clay lazily pointed his arm at a blonde girl running at X and shot. "Others group together and live in one place, only moving from there to forage. This is only a fraction of them all."

Yet it felt like the onslaught of attackers never ended. My arms were heavy, my fingers bleeding from shrapnel. By the time I shot at the final person, I was barely able to stand. The tech was intelligent enough to work without me knowing what I was doing, but it did sap my energy somehow. Maybe I was one big walking battery for it.

Clay grinned at me. "We did it. Actually did it."

The last bit of strength left me, and I let myself drop from the tree, landing on all fours next to a corpse. Dead eyes stared at me accusingly. Until that moment, it had all been a surreal game.

Not anymore. I had killed. I had taken a life. Several. And I hadn't even felt any kind of remorse at the time.

I gagged, bile rising in my throat.

I was a killer.

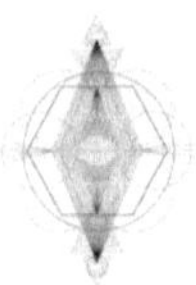

11

The aliens had won. They'd taken my humanity. They'd turned me into their weapon.

"Eileen," Kenny said gently from behind me. "You didn't have a choice."

He put a hand on my shoulder, but I shrugged him off. "Didn't I?"

I stumbled to my feet and started walking, away from those accusing dead eyes, from the bloody corpses, from the men who were shouting for me to stay.

"I need some time," I told them without looking back.

They'd been here for longer. They'd killed goodness knew how many people. X and Y had murdered other humans in front of my eyes back at the lake. Now, I really was one of them.

Not that they'd had any more choice in this than I'd had. We were forced to become murderers. Killing was the only way to survive. And it was nobody's fault, other than the aliens'.

"Tim!" I shouted, clenching my fists as a wave of rage

overcame me. It gave me strength, enough to stand up straight as I waited for him to respond.

"You fought well. I watched the battle. Your vitals are a little off, are you hurt?"

If he'd been here, I'd have spat at him.

"Hurt? My heart has been torn into pieces, but I doubt you'd care about that. You made me kill people. You turned me into a monster."

He sighed. "I told you to run. Remember? It was you who decided to stay and fight."

"Because my friends were in danger! I couldn't just leave them!"

He sighed. "And that is your choice. All of this has been your choice. They even asked you if you were sure you wanted to do this when you went through the gate. Blame me if it makes you feel better, but what you did—and you did well—you did yourself by your own choice. You want those four to be your people in there? Fine. They're yours. I'll help you as best I can, but if you don't want to listen to me, if you won't run when I tell you to, then you'll fight. That's how this works."

I had to catch my breath. He wasn't fucking wrong, and that made this even worse. I had chosen all of this. Maybe I hadn't had all the information I needed, but no one had held a gun to my head and told me to go through the gate. Tim had told me to run. I hadn't. And now I'd killed a whole bunch of people with the technology inside of me. I was a murderer, and if I wanted to stay alive, and potentially keep these guys that I really liked that way, too, I was going to have to somehow survive being this person.

I wiped tears from my cheeks.

"Eileen," Blake said, and I turned to him. He stood with Kenny.

I sniffed. I'd asked for a moment, but the truth was that I didn't mind the company. Not now that Tim wasn't going to let me hide from this being absolutely my own fault. I wiped my eyes again. "Sorry, guys, crying. Give me a minute. I'll stop."

Kenny tugged me to him. "You can cry. I used to cry. Maybe that's not... I don't know... macho. But I'll admit it. A million years ago. I used to cry."

I laughed. "In a million years, I guess I'll stop, too."

He pressed his nose in my hair. "I knew when you woke up in that cage, when I was there, that you were going to be really important in my life. It's why I followed you around."

I closed my eyes. I had to pull it together. "We have to get our handlers to all cooperate with each other."

Suddenly, the sun set in the sky. One second it was up, the next it was down. The suddenness of it jarred me, and I grabbed onto Kenny, reaching for the others, too. Peter appeared, still not talking, and Clay was there by his side.

"That usual?"

Clay sighed. "Nope. But I think we'd better take shelter."

I touched my ear. "Tim?"

"'I'm here. Clay's right. Take shelter. They want to test the swimming tech. They're going to flood the place."

I gasped. "Flood?"

"Fuck." Peter found his voice. This time, they must not have jarred him for it.

These guys were still beat up. I hadn't gone through all of that to keep them alive in order to have them drown.

"Tell me about your tech for swimming, guys. Who has any?"

Kenny raised his hand. "I do, but I'm not sure how up to

date it is. That's why my handler wanted me to go swim in the lake."

Peter and Blake both shook their heads, but Clay grinned. "Me, too. Top notch. I can breathe underwater for around five minutes. You don't want to know how I found out, but let's be glad that I know. I'm fast, too."

"You've got the same tech," Tim said in my head. "Slightly upgraded. Ten minutes underwater, plus flippers on your feet."

I froze. "Flippers? How the hell do I have flippers?"

I was tempted to take my boots off to check, but I knew that there were no scars on my feet. No new ones, anyway.

Tim chuckled. If only I could get to him and slap him for taking this as a joke. "You should have realized by now that our technology is vastly superior to anything you know. There are tiny folded flippers embedded in the soles of your feet, taking the space of some flesh we removed. They break through the skin and expand when needed."

"You took my... flesh?" I was speechless. That alien really was entirely inhuman.

"Amongst other things," he said dryly. "You never asked how long you were unconscious after you first woke up. It took a while to regenerate your skin where we added the tech and removed unnecessary things, but you should be grateful we're that advanced by now. The first people in the game looked a lot less... healthy."

I shuddered. Tim was giving me answers I didn't want to hear.

"What's your alien saying?" Blake asked, and I remembered that they couldn't hear Tim, only my responses.

"That I'm Frankenstein's monster, basically. But let's find shelter before we all drown."

Kenny pointed toward the last sliver of sun that was barely illuminating our surroundings. "If they've not changed everything, we should get to a small hill that way. If they flood the place, that's the highest point I know of, so we might be safe there."

I shielded my eyes and looked at where he was pointing but couldn't see anything besides empty, flat ground. "If there's a hill, it's far away."

"Then we better get moving." Kenny gave me a crazed grin and started walking, not looking back. I exchanged a look with the other guys, but since none of us had any better ideas, we followed Kenny, leaving the bodies of the dead behind.

WALKING through the night was scary. Every sound in the distance made me jump. Were there reapers out there? Spider monsters? Worse creatures than even those? My eyes were surprisingly good at seeing in the dark. Probably a tech thing, although I really didn't want to imagine the aliens messing with my eyes. What part of me was still the old Eileen? How much of me was left?

"I hate the darkness," Peter growled to my right. "If only we had stars, but they removed those a few months ago. Made it too easy to orient ourselves."

"Is that a house over there? Maybe if we warn the occupants of the flood, they'll let us on the roof." I sounded ridiculous to my own ears.

Clay shook his head. "They're just as likely to kill us. We're just going to have to take the roof by force."

I gritted my teeth. I supposed it was too much to ask that the occupants of that house had already died in the killing I'd had to do earlier. "Tim? Any chance its empty?"

"Nope." He didn't have much to say. Why was it that sometimes it was like pulling teeth, and sometimes he couldn't say enough? I shook my head. Who knew with Tim. Half the time, he only wanted to talk about science.

All right, we had to fight.

Just then, a woman stumbled outside, her hands raised. The guys immediately pointed their tech at her. I looked between them. "It's one woman with her hands raised. I think you'll be fi-"

I never got to finish that thought. She pointed her tech at me and fired. She'd have hit me, too, if Clay hadn't thrown me onto the ground.

I groaned, hearing gun fire sound all around me. With my open hand, I pounded on the ground.

"Trying to die?" Tim sounded annoyed.

"No, obviously not." I winced.

The gunfire stopped, and Clay hauled me to my feet. "Don't stand there while someone tries to shoot you, or your handler will start taking over your fights. Trust me, that hurts worse."

I stared at the dead woman on the ground. A pool of blood floated out around her. The drones would be here later to remove the mess. That's all we were to them once we were dead. Mess.

We approached the house, hands outstretched, a lot more wary this time. I should have known by now that looks could be deceiving. People had underestimated me all my life, just like I had misjudged the woman.

Clay took the lead, and I let him. My skin still tingled where he'd lain on top of me, even though it had just been for a few seconds.

The door to the house stood open, but Clay motioned for the others to walk around the house and check for other exits. I stayed with him while the others snuck off, hoping that there was nobody else in the house who we might have to kill. The death toll was rising rapidly, and that was before the promised flooding.

"I don't think anyone's inside," Tim whispered in my head, as if he didn't want to startle me. How very considerate. It didn't make me want to strangle him any less.

Suddenly, the ground began to tremble. A strange rumbling sound filled the air, coming from underneath.

"Go inside!" Clay shouted. "We need to get on the roof before the water comes."

He rushed in, and I followed him, my arms extended just in case someone hostile was waiting for us. I didn't even look around and went straight for the narrow staircase. Footsteps behind reassured me that the other guys had followed Clay's command and abandoned their sneaking around. Another staircase, then we were on the top floor. No hatch leading to an attic. Panic spread through me. This may have been a trap.

"Spread out, search the rooms," I huffed breathlessly. "We need to find a way up to the roof."

I went straight ahead, ending up in a small bedroom so full of dust that I couldn't help but sneeze. The ceiling was bare, save for a dirty lampshade. We'd not get to the attic from here. I returned to the hallway.

"Nothing," Peter groaned. "We're trapped. We don't want the attic. People drown that way."

"Same in the bathroom and bedroom," his brother confirmed.

Clay shook his head, his expression grave. Kenny hadn't returned yet, having disappeared down the corridor.

"Kenny? Any luck?" I shouted, crossing both fingers and toes.

"No," a faint call came back. "But I found food."

That wasn't going to help us. Having something to eat wasn't very high on my list of priorities just now. The trembling was steadily becoming stronger, and the walls around us were creaking under the strain. Something was happening, and I doubted it was going to be a rescue operation.

"We need to go outside," Clay voiced my own thoughts. "If the water hits us here, we might not get out in time."

A loud bang followed his words as the door downstairs was pushed open. The house shuddered, and the sound of waves hitting stone made my heart pound in fear.

"Too late," Blake whispered. "The water's arrived."

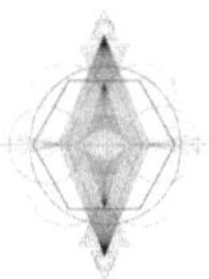

12

We were going to drown inside of this house. I stepped back, lifting my hand. I really hoped that I had the right explosives inside of me.

"Tim, I'm going to blow up the wall."

There was a pause. "On it. You're fully charged."

That was great. Blake yanked Clay back from me just as a small projectile launched itself from my hand. I cried out. Man... that hurt. I looked down. Black soot marred my skin, and it had burned me.

"Fuck, sorry, Eileen. That's a mistake. It shouldn't hurt you."

I shook my head. "Everything hurts me. Come on, guys, we need to get out of here before the water rises so high, we can't."

Peter grinned. "Looks like we're going for a swim."

He really was a little sick in the head. But I guessed we all were at this point. I rushed through the hole I'd made. It seemed crazy to be going toward the water, but in this house, the only thing we were going to do was drown. It had been a good thought, but the designers of this place had clearly not wanted to make a roof access.

I dived into the water, my flippers coming out of my feet. Why hadn't he given me that ability when I'd been in the lake? Well, fuck if I knew. Tim did things in his own way, and I couldn't make hide nor hair out of it.

I surfaced fast, kicking my feet swifter than I would have on my own. I could feel the mechanics.

"Well done," Tim sighed. "Did you say all the tech hurts you?"

He was still on that? "Yes."

"Shit. Well, that's not good."

Really? He was telling me? I was the one feeling the pain.

The world around us was flooded. Why would they have created the new landscape just to cover it in water? Nothing made sense anymore. Blake appeared right next to me. Clay after him, and soon, Kenny and Peter were with us.

Kenny grinned. "I used to love to swim when I was a kid. My dad would take me to the lake and tell me stories of the world before the aliens came and we all started to starve to death. Haven't thought of that in years." He paused. "Could be making that up. You know the background thing. I think...I mean I might not have had family."

He floated on his back. Well, at least one of us could make the most of this even if he was very confused. I...

Dread filled me as I saw what was right behind. There was a fucking fin.

"Kenny!" I shouted.

"Shark!" Clay yelled at the same time.

The fin was too shiny to be that of a real animal.

Probably another metal monster like the spiders. That only made it worse.

The water was rising quickly, but the roof was still poking out of the newly created sea. Without having to coordinate, we all started swimming toward it as fast as we could. My flippers propelled me through the water, and Clay managed to just about keep up with me, but the others weren't equipped with the same tech. I looked back, cringing as I watched the pointed fin circle us. It could have attacked already, but it seemed to be waiting. Stalking us. Playing with its food. Who knew how much farther the water would rise? The roof might be only a short reprieve before we were stranded in the open water. I cursed the aliens for putting us through this. Couldn't they just have built a weapons range like any sane person? I supposed this was more entertaining for them. Watching humans be killed. And killing each other.

Something touched my foot, and I shrieked, kicking out at whatever was in the water beneath me.

Blake screamed, and I turned back to him just in time to see his head disappear beneath the surface. Peter was by his side, both of them slow because they didn't have any tech that could help them. He met my eyes then dived.

"Kenny, Clay, get to the roof," I spluttered, a wave hitting me unexpectedly. "I'm the strongest of us."

Surprisingly, they listened to me, swimming toward the house. I took the opposite direction, willing my tech to get me to Blake in time. Peter resurfaced to take a breath, shook his head, and dived again. My heart beat painfully in my chest. The shark fin was no longer to be seen, which likely meant that the monster had taken Blake. Fuck.

When I got close to where Blake had been pulled under, I dived, not surprised at all that I could see perfectly. Dark shadows moved beneath me, at least a dozen or so. There wasn't just one monster to deal with. There was an entire pack of them. A shape swam toward me, and I pointed my arm at it but then breathed in relief when I realized it was Peter. He had his eyes closed, unable to see me. I let him swim toward the surface to breathe. Something I didn't need to do. For once, I was grateful for my tech. Breathing down here felt natural, not at all as if I was sucking water into my lungs. No, I wasn't. I touched the side of my neck. I had fucking gills. I'd wanted them, but fuck if it wasn't a lot to take in. It hadn't hurt this time, but maybe that was due to the cooling water.

I dived deeper, my arm pointed at the shadows just in case one of them decided to attack me. There was no sign of Blake. Please, don't let it be too late. I couldn't lose him.

Then, finally, I spotted him, limp in the jaws of a massive metal shark. Blake wasn't moving. That much I could see right off the bat. Blood seeped from his head and floated slowly around him. His eyes were closed. He was either dead or going to be.

My heart fell into my stomach. No, I wasn't going to lose him. I dived toward him, a spear suddenly launching from my arm. I hadn't fired it. That meant it had to be Tim. Thank you, I silently sent his way. It hit the shark in the eye. The robot darted left and right, letting go of Blake, who floated down.

I swam fast, grabbing him and launching us both for the surface as fast as I could manage. We made it to air, but by the time we did, I knew for certain he wasn't breathing. I swam hard. Hands—Clay's—darted out, grabbing Blake and pulling him onto the roof.

"Fuck," Peter shouted.

I didn't have time to pay attention. I actually knew CPR. My father taught me, years and years ago.

I pumped on his chest. Thirty compressions. Two breaths. Repeat. Again. I pressed my lips to his, blowing air into him. I knew what I was doing. The others said things, they shouted. Peter might have cried. I couldn't really hear them. They were like background noise. One. Two. Three.

Come on, Blake. Don't leave me now.

Water came out of his mouth, followed by a gasp and a violent cough. Over and over. Tears exploded from my eyes, and I bent my head. Okay. He wasn't dead. He wasn't dead. He...

Arms came around me. Kenny. He kissed my cheek. "You saved him. You did it."

I nodded. I guessed I had.

Peter helped Blake sit up, and although he'd been dead only minutes earlier, he hugged me, too. "Thank you." His throat sounded scratchy, but it was the best sound in the world. Peter joined the hug. Then Clay. We all shook together. There was nothing to do except be there in that moment, as we all knew what might have been.

Peter met my gaze. He swallowed, and I nodded. Words didn't matter. Not right then.

⁕

I sat with Blake's head in my lap. He slept, and I counted his breaths like he might stop at any time. My hands were in his hair. Next to me, Kenny snored. Peter dozed by my head, and to my left, Clay lay on his side, breathing deeply. I didn't know how any of them rested after what happened.

The water hadn't gotten any higher. At least not yet.

"Well done," Tim said in my ear, and I smiled.

"Thanks for the assist." In this case, I absolutely couldn't have done it without him.

"Listen, I talked to others, and we may have a solution. After the flood, there are only six other people left. I think they mean to replace all of you with newer models. If you—the five of you—can take out the six remaining, we will support you. All five of you together."

That couldn't be the end of it. "And?"

"Then you'll have to take out each other. But until then... you can stay together."

I couldn't answer that alone. "I'll need to talk to the others."

"Yep. Keep in mind, it's this or the demo continues, and you're immediately ready to kill each other. Those are the only two options."

I looked up at the sky. "This is hell."

"No, Eileen. This is Purgatory. Trust me. Hell is yet to come."

He wasn't joking. Worse things were going to happen. More deaths. More suffering. It was a miracle that we were all still alive. Living until the day we were forced to kill each other by the tech forced into our bodies without our knowledge.

"What did your alien say?" Peter asked, and I forced myself to look less conflicted than I felt.

"There are six other humans left alive," I reported. "He wants us to kill them."

Clay blinked at me, tiredness reflecting in his eyes. "What if this is a trick? To provide more entertainment for them?"

"Yeah, we don't know how many there really are. It could be a trap," Peter added, rubbing the back of his neck. "They might want to see us all die."

I shook my head. "He sounded sincere. I trust him, at least enough to think that he's not wanting me to get killed."

"You've got a strange relationship with your handler." Blake had woken up and was looking at me with a wary expression on his face. "I'm not sure it's healthy."

"Sometimes, it's better to get to know your enemy."

"Hey, I heard that," Tim complained in my head. "I hope you don't really think that. I'm not your enemy. I'm the best ally you've got."

I snorted. "Ally? You've put tech into me that I didn't want. You made me kill people I didn't want to kill. You put me into this situation, and you want me to see you as a friend?" I laughed coldly. "No way. If you want to be my ally, come down here and show yourself. Help us get out of this place, alive. Then I might reconsider our relationship."

"I see." His voice was clipped. "I thought we'd moved further than that."

"Then you thought wrong," I snapped.

Clay yawned, opening his eyes. "Trouble in paradise?"

"Trouble in hell," I retorted. "Sleep well?"

He smiled happily. "I had the most amazing dream. A seal swam up to me, and when it reached the beach, she transformed into a beautiful woman. She looked just like you, Eileen. And then we fucked on the beach while the sun set on the horizon."

Peter laughed. "Very romantic. Or is that just a pickup line and not actually a dream?"

Clay reached out to me and put a hand on my thigh. "It was a dream, but I'd be happy to make it reality."

"Except for the seal part," I quipped. "I don't think my tech extends that far."

We fell quiet, staring out over the water that had swallowed the world. It was a strangely peaceful sight, now that it had stopped rising. A few puffed up clouds reflected on the smooth surface. Our roof was the only thing still standing, the only color in the landscape besides some debris floating in the water. The world was going to be a very muddy place once the water was drained. Would they use the underground tunnels to get rid of it all? Likely. Thank goodness we were no longer down there. We would have drowned for sure.

Clay got up and walked to the edge of the roof, holding his hands together to pour some water into his mouth. "Think positive. It could have been salt water."

He looked so happy that I couldn't help but smile. It was admirable how he could see the positive about our current predicament. We were trapped on a roof, soaked, without food, but at least we had as much drinking water as we wanted. Somehow, I had a feeling that the next thing the aliens threw at us would be a desert.

Blake had fallen back asleep, while Kenny was still snoring softly. I wished I could sleep, too. I was exhausted, but I knew my mind was going to refuse to shut off until we were in a safer place.

"I kind of want to be him," Peter whispered, his gaze burning into mine. "My head in your lap, your hands in my hair. It sounds like paradise. A tiny piece of paradise in the middle of Hell."

"Purgatory," I corrected, a blush spreading across my cheeks. "Tim said Hell is yet to come."

"Doesn't matter. Next time, I want to be the one who gets rescued."

I shook my head. "I don't want there to be a reason you have to be rescued." I leaned over, trying to not jar Blake, and kissed Peter. He sighed against my mouth.

It would be easy to just forget right this moment. I had

four very good-looking men who all wanted me. I could pretend I didn't have an alien in my ear complicating things. We could just all... be. Well, they could all *be* with me. I didn't get the impression they wanted to *be* with each other. Although that might have been sort of hot to watch. I shook my head. My thoughts were getting away from me.

Peter pressed his lips closer and this time, it was my turn to sigh.

He pulled back to whisper in my ear. "I know your alien can hear me, and I don't care. Listen to me, I won't kill you. When it comes to the end, I won't. You're the first bright light I've had in my life. You saved my brother's life. As far as I'm concerned, you're some sort of fucking reward I got for surviving this long, and I'm not sure I deserve you. So, we'll take out those six, but know that when it comes down to it, I'm not killing you. And if you can hear me, handler that she calls Tim, I'm not killing her. Aim your tech at me. I'm not firing back. Even if my handler tries to push it."

I shuddered. Those weren't words he should have to say. I cupped his face. "I'm going to hope beyond hope, beyond reason that somehow, there can be another way."

He nodded. "Me, too." He kissed me one more time before he put his head on my shoulder. I didn't know how long we were going to all stay like this, but I was grateful for the time. There was nothing we could do until the water drained.

Blake jolted awake. He blinked into consciousness. "Sorry, I guess I fell back asleep."

I shook my head. "You need the rest. You were dead. I know the tech helps us, but you've got to need to sleep."

He lowered his head again. "I'm not having great dreams."

Since there was nothing to say, I didn't remark. Clay sat down behind me, and a second later, he rubbed my back.

"So then we kill them." He finally said. "And we worry about what happens next then. One thing at a time. Tell Tim we'll do it. Mine isn't talking to me."

"Tim? You get that?"

He sighed. "Yep, I hear you. Eileen... there are so many things I wish I could tell you. Please know there was once a time I was you. Okay? We were where you were once. Our own equivalent of it. I never got to have moments like you're getting to have. I get why you can't be my friend. But I am on your side."

Who was *we*? I almost asked him, and then I didn't. Why would I do that? I didn't need to know Tim any more than I did. The only point to any of this was on this roof. They were mine. Peter said he wouldn't kill me, well, I wouldn't hurt him either. I just wasn't going to announce for whoever else watched to know.

Kenny lifted his head. "Hey, guys."

I smiled at him. "Hey, there. Welcome to it. We're going to kill six people and then have to kill each other."

My craziest guy nodded. "Just another day in paradise."

[13]

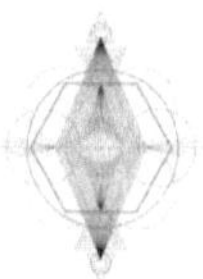

Slowly, the water began to disappear. Yes, that's exactly what it did. Instead of the water gauge gently lowering like I'd expected, it turned into thick white mist, hiding the surrounding landscape from us. We camped out on the roof, wet and hungry, until the mist finally started to retreat in the early hours of the morning. It was a beautiful sight, to be honest. Crimson light shone upon the last whiffs of fog clinging to the ground. It didn't seem to be as muddy as I had anticipated. We might be able to walk away from here without drowning in mud like quicksand.

First though, we had to get off the roof. Now that the water had gone, we were an awfully long distance away from the ground. Jumping would hurt. A lot. Unless the aliens had put dampers in my legs that would buffer the impact.

"We could take our clothes off and knot them into a rope," Kenny suggested, looking straight at me.

"You want me to strip?"

"It's the perfect excuse to show off your body, wouldn't

you say?" He gave me a grin that would have seemed innocent, if not for the crazed twinkle in his eyes.

"You just want to see me naked."

He nodded. "Yes. Exactly."

"I agree," Clay chuckled, his gaze roaming up and down my chest. "It would cheer us up a lot."

"I'm not going to show you my boobs just to make you happy. We have more important things to do."

Like killing people, I completed the sentence in my head. I didn't speak those words though. They were hard enough to think.

I inspected the roof. Maybe Kenny was right about making a rope. But where would we even tie it? There was nothing strong enough to hold our weight.

Peter groaned. "We should have gone into the water when it was still close to the roof. It would have made it so much easier."

I doubted that would work. They'd have found some way to mess with us. I was surprised that he was still able to talk that much. His handler was either not watching or didn't care any longer. Blake was half-asleep, still recovering from his ordeal. We'd know soon if he was allowed to speak or not.

At least no water meant no sharks. We were back to spiders and reapers, most likely. Or maybe the aliens kept those creatures away, now that it was human against human.

I walked around the roof, looking for a weak spot that might give us access to the attic below. Nothing. I should have known, after all, it was strong enough to carry five people and survive being an island in an ocean.

I glared at the men who were all watching me, even Blake. "All right. Clothes off."

"Wait," Tim said in my head. For once, I was happy to hear him. "Give me a second, I've just been given access to a drone. It'll be there in a moment. Don't attack it, it's under my control."

"Keep your clothes on," I told the others, but Peter had already taken his shirt off, exposing a deliciously sculpted chest. "Tim is sending a drone."

I scoured the sky, and yes, there was a tiny silver dot in the distance, rapidly becoming larger. Sunlight reflected on its metal surface, making it bright as a star. Beautiful. Until it came closer and reminded me of our time below the surface, when the drones had carried in Clay and Kenny.

"Hold onto the bar attached to the belly of the drone, and it will carry you down one by one," Tim instructed. I relayed his words to the others.

"Sure we can trust him?" Clay asked. "What if he's only going to carry you down and then drop us? It would be an easy way for him to kill us without you having to dirty your hands."

It was clear he didn't suspect me of wanting that. Only Tim. They didn't trust him. I hadn't either... but in this moment, I realized that I did. I knew in my heart that he wanted to help me. Protect me. He may have been an alien, but my instincts told me that he was speaking the truth.

"He's going to save us all. But to prove it, one of you go first."

I stood and waited. Blake got to his feet. "I'm in pretty bad shape. As I'm going to be the one to slow us down, I'll go first in case it goes badly. I'm the weakest link right now."

I shook my head. "Sweetheart, don't talk about yourself like that."

His smile was huge. "That's my nickname now. None of the rest of them get to be sweetheart."

He grabbed onto the drone, and it took him to the ground gently before it returned for the rest of us. Peter went next, followed by Clay, leaving Kenny and me on the roof alone.

I pointed to the waiting drone. "Now you."

"No." He cupped my cheek. "You go. I'm not leaving you up here to be last. What if some vulture swoops down from the sky? You go."

I wouldn't even be surprised if that happened. "I'll feel better if you go. Tim will take care of me. I trust him."

"Thank you for that," my handler spoke in my ear. "After our last conversation, I didn't think you felt that way. There are no vultures coming. However, the six remaining living souls will be on you guys in half an hour."

I pointed again. "Half an hour till we fight. Go down. Please."

Kenny kissed me hard. I melted against him. "Trust the alien all you want. But know that we have your back for sure. When he lets you down, I won't. I've played this game a long time, paid out every ounce of my soul, or so I thought, because I walked through that gate. Then you came. I won't be killing you. I don't care who hears it. When we reach the end, you're going to still be standing, Eileen."

He grabbed onto the drone.

"They're very loyal to you, that's for sure." Tim sighed. "And it's not about you being a woman. They've met lots of women. They see in you what we see, too. You're up. Get off that roof. Stay alive."

That was the goal. With his words in my mind and the word *we* hanging out there, I took the drone all the way to the ground. The strange deadly part of my life was about to come to an end.

One way or another.

"Should we stay here and barricade ourselves in the house?" I asked as soon as my feet touched the ground.

"Don't," Tim said in my head before any of the guys could answer. "They want this to be a proper, outdoor battle, and they're going to make sure they get it. The house isn't safe, not with all the game controllers watching."

"Is that different from a handler?"

Tim didn't reply.

I sighed. Getting helpful answers from him was as difficult as finding a place of safety in this forsaken land.

The drone had been hovering nearby until now, but with a beep, it flew off, leaving us alone. Not that I had any illusions about there being people watching us. Aliens looking forward to seeing us die. Bastards.

"Let's move away from here," I said. "Maybe we'll find a place where we can make a stand."

❖

I touched Blake's cheek. He was hot. It would really be awful for us to have gotten all this way to lose Blake to infection.

"Two minutes."

A very wet, slightly torn apart tree stood in front of us. I looked over at Blake. "Go up it, please. Give us cover from up there, but don't fight."

"I'm bad off, aren't I? My handler's gone silent."

I leaned over and kissed his cheek. "Just be careful."

Peter helped Blake up the tree while I took in our surroundings. The ground had dried into a desert full of cracks and strange mud formations. A few boulders in the distance seemed the best place to ambush the other humans. I hated how I was making plans on how best to kill them. I wasn't a murderer. Yet it was the only way. Short of letting them kill us first. And I had to protect the guys.

Blake blended in well, barely standing out amongst the tree's sparse foliage. Good, hopefully he'd be able to stay safe and unseen.

"To the stones."

They followed me. When had I become the leader? I didn't care. This was about survival. We'd sort out our relationship if we managed to escape this hell.

"One minute." Tim sounded tense.

I broke into a run, the others close behind. Those boulders would give us a bit of shelter, but I was sure it wasn't going to be enough. The chances of all of us surviving were small.

I crouched behind the biggest stone and turned back, looking at the men. Who of them would still be alive an hour from now? I hadn't known them for long, yet I couldn't bear the idea of losing one of them.

"Don't look so worried," Kenny chuckled. "You look like you're about to pee yourself."

I glared at him. "Not the time."

"My handler just told me goodbye," Clay interrupted, his eyes wide. "I think this is it. They really expect us to die."

A shiver ran down my back. If our handlers didn't even believe that we'd survive, then what hope was there? Death was about to meet us, and I so wasn't ready.

"We can do this," I whispered. "We'll get through this. We'll survive. All of us."

Kenny put a hand on my shoulder. "Dying will be fun, you'll see."

His eyes were more crazed than I'd ever seen. He was about to break.

"We're not going to die," Peter said firmly. "And if we do, we protect Eileen, is that understood?"

I stared at him in surprise. His whole demeanor had changed from one second to the next. Gone was the man who barely spoke. The way he held his shoulders, the steel in his eyes, the way he stared us down... I thought I could see a glimpse of the man he used to be. Someone strong, someone in charge. Someone who thrived in the face of danger.

"Yes, sir." Clay bowed his head, obviously feeling the same authority transmitted by Peter.

"You don't need to protect me," I interjected. "I've got the best tech out of all of us. I'll—"

I never got to finish my sentence. Something hit the ground next to me and exploded. I was thrown through the air, and everything went crazy.

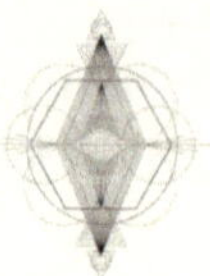

Dust filled the air, my eyes, my nose. A high-pitched ringing pierced my ears, but it was already getting quieter. I coughed and spat out the foul taste in my mouth. Shots rang in the distance, but I couldn't see through all the dust.

I wanted to shout out for the others, find out if they were okay, but instinct told me to stay quiet. I didn't know where our attackers were, and I didn't want to give my position away just yet. They seemed to have better tech at their disposal than us. What had that even been, a bomb, a grenade? Let's hope they only had one of those.

"Everyone's still alive," Tim whispered in my head, as if he didn't want to startle me. "So are your enemies."

That was reassuring. I'd not lost any of my friends yet. There was still time to eliminate our foes before they did the same to us.

My eye itched, and I blinked. Without warning, my vision changed. Colors drained from the landscape, their place taken by deep grays and blacks. And there, in the distance, a bright red figure, female, her arms outstretched as if she was preparing to attack.

I took a deep breath and pointed my own arms at her. I'd never tried to attack anyone this far away, but getting closer wasn't an option. Hopefully, I was the only one with this strange enhanced vision.

I still had no idea how I actually controlled this tech, if that was even possible. I just wished it to happen and hoped for the best. Something shot from my right arm.

It hit the woman right in the chest, and she staggered back, but she didn't go down as I'd hoped. Fuck. Now she knew where I was. She rubbed her chest with one hand while pointing the other right at me. My body reacted before my mind could catch up. I dived to the right, hitting the dusty ground hard. Behind me, an explosion sounded, caused by whatever the woman had thrown at me. She really wasn't taking any prisoners.

This time, my ears didn't ring, as if my tech had adapted to the deafening noises. I looked around for my men, but the dust concealed everything. The second explosion had thrown up even more dirt, and hopefully, the woman had lost sight of me.

I got up in a crouch and moved away from the scene, hoping I'd randomly stumble across one of the guys and not an enemy.

"Where are they?" I whispered, but Tim didn't respond.

My throat was bone dry, and with every breath full of dust I sucked into my lungs, the urge to cough increased. But that could give me away. I had to be quiet. Stealthy.

The ground shook as more explosions hit all around me. Those other humans were so much better equipped than us. I had the most advanced tech out of all of us, and yet, I wasn't able to make things explode. At least, I didn't think so. Maybe it was time to try.

Shapes appeared in the distance, but I couldn't make out if they were friend or foe. Well, if they were the guys, I'd want to be with them. If they were enemies, I had to take them out, even though I wanted to retch at the thought of having to kill.

I crept closer, ready to shoot if they were the other humans. And yes. A man and a woman. They were both wearing strange long coats, despite the heat. Definitely not my guys.

I took a deep breath and aimed. My arms were shaking. They hadn't attacked me. It wasn't like with the woman earlier. She'd shot at me first, and I'd only defended myself. This time, I was going to have to shoot first. I hated the aliens for what they were making me do. They were turning me into a monster.

"You can do it," I whispered to myself. "You don't have a choice."

Hearing the words helped somehow.

I willed my tech to do as much damage as possible, aimed, and mentally released the trigger. A lance of fire shot from my left arm, searing my skin and making me cry out in pain. From my right hand, bullets flew, old-fashioned but effective. Both missiles hit their targets. The man went down without a sound, the bullets embedded in his chest. The woman wavered, staring down at the flames spreading across her body. Then she screamed.

I averted my eyes. She was burning alive, and it was my doing. The smell of seared flesh reached my nose, and this time, I couldn't help but retch. Bile rose up in my throat, and I spit it out, almost relishing the burning sensation in my mouth. It was my punishment. I had just killed two people.

That meant there might still be four enemies left. The woman with the bombs and three others. I still hadn't seen any of my men, either. I both wanted and didn't want the dust to settle. It would expose us, but it would let me find out if the guys were still alive.

"Tim?" I whispered again.

Silence. Had my tech been damaged, or did he just refuse to answer? Maybe he'd been forbidden to talk. There seemed to be a lot going on wherever he was. Alliances, orders, secrets.

I didn't have time to worry about Tim. The explosions had stopped. Hopefully, that meant the woman was dead. I berated myself for the thought. Yet it was true. I needed her to be dead, even though that was a life taken for no reason but to save my own. And that of the guys.

With the dust slowly getting less, I stayed close to the ground, moving randomly across our makeshift battlefield. I'd lost all sense of place. The boulders had to be somewhere, but I couldn't for the life of me remember in which direction. Not that hiding was an option.

Suddenly, something hit me from behind. A body. Hands wrapped around my throat and squeezed. Panic filled me, made me freeze up. I couldn't breathe. Fight, you have to fight. I held my breath, pretended that it was my choice not to breathe, not that of the man who was strangling me.

Everything went very clear. My mind became cold, calculating. I remembered the way I'd fought off X—Blake— at the very beginning. Prosynchronic wave, that's what they'd called it. Back then, Tim had initiated it, but there had to be a way for me to set it off. That was the point of having all this tech embedded in us.

I imagined how it had felt to have all that energy released from my body. How light had filled my eyes. How Blake had been thrown off me.

And then it happened. Just like that. My body buckled beneath the man, and he flew through the air, thrown by an unseen force.

I gasped for breath. If I'd thought my throat was sore before, that had been nothing against the pain I was experiencing now.

I scrambled to my feet as fast as I could, pointing my hands at the man, but he was on the ground, lifeless. I approached him cautiously. He could have been faking it. I wished I still had my bow. Shooting from a distance would have been so much simpler. And safer.

I prodded the man with my foot. He didn't move. There was no way around it. I kneeled by his side and put my hands against his throat, taking his pulse. None. I waited for at least a minute, dreading that his heart might restart, but he stayed dead.

That made three people I'd killed in one day. If I believed in an afterlife, I'd go to Hell for sure. Sadly, I was already in Hell while being still alive.

A scream cut through the silence. Clay.

I didn't think. I ran toward the shout as fast as I could, no longer caring about stealth. Now that the dust was almost completely settled, moving was a lot faster.

Clay was on the ground, surrounded by two other bodies. Peter was kneeling by his side, his hands on Clay's chest. There was blood everywhere. Fuck. Fuck. Fuck.

I skidded to a halt and fell to my knees, taking in the

scene. Clay's eyes were closed, his skin a sickly pallor. Peter looked up and gave me a short nod.

"He was hit by shrapnel. The wound is pretty deep. I've been trying to stem the flow, but I don't have anything to treat him with."

There were bloody fingerprints on his face, but it didn't seem to be his blood.

"Are you hurt?" I asked, relieved when he shook his head.

"Just a few scrapes. You?"

"No. Have you seen the others?"

"Only Kenny. He was laughing while randomly shooting in the air. I think he's gone completely crazy."

I put a hand on Clay's forehead. He was too cold, too clammy.

"Tim!" I shouted. "We need help."

No response. If that bastard could hear me and just didn't want to help, I was going to kill him.

"Do you know how many there are left?"

He shook his head, then nodded toward the two bodies behind me. "Clay killed one of them, me the other."

"I killed three. That means there might still be one left. Or maybe more. Or maybe not. I can't... I'm not sure."

I took a closer look at the bodies. Both men.

"There was a woman, the one who threw all those bombs. I shot at her, but it didn't seem to have any effect."

"Yes, I saw her," Peter confirmed. "But then I got thrown back in an explosion and lost sight of her."

Clay groaned, and despite the sound scraping at my heart, I was relieved to see his eyelids flutter open.

"Clay, can you hear me?"

I kept my hand on his forehead, gently pushing his hair back.

"Eileen." His voice was a whisper. "You're alive."

"I am. And you will live, too, if I have anything to say about it."

"Angel," he muttered.

I sighed. "Definitely not an angel. I killed three people. Shot at another."

"Angel," he repeated.

"Eileen," Peter said sharply. "Behind you."

I turned around – and gasped. An angel was walking toward us. A man with large, metal wings that glinted in the sun. His face was hidden in shadow, concealing whether he was human or something else entirely.

"What the fuck..."

I got up, staring at the angel. Was he here to rescue us from Purgatory?

He reached out with one arm, pointing at me with his index finger. Light began to pool around his hand, beautiful and mesmerizing. I couldn't stop looking at the beautiful apparition. With the sun behind him, illuminating his wings, he really looked like a heavenly creature. Here to help us. Our salvation.

I reached out for him as he came closer. The light around his hand became brighter, all consuming.

Suddenly, I was pushed aside as someone jumped at me from the left. We tumbled to the ground just as the angel released a massive lightning bolt from his hand. Heat seared my skin. If I'd still stood where I'd been, I was sure there'd be a gaping burned hole in my chest. My rescuer was still on top of me, pushing me to the ground.

A cackle broke the shocked silence. Kenny. It was Kenny. He jumped to his feet and shot at the angel while laughing wildly. The angel wrapped his wings around his body like metal armor, reflecting the bullets shooting from

Kenny's hands. They were easily repelled by the wings, harmlessly falling to the ground.

The angel roared and suddenly, he wasn't all that angelic anymore. He turned a little, letting light shine on his face, and I could finally see him properly. He was just a man. Scars lined his weathered face, speaking of many struggles in the past. He stretched out his arm, pointing at Kenny, lightning pooling around his hand once again, but this time I wasn't taken in.

By holding out his arm, he was exposing a part of his chest that wasn't covered by his wings. I aimed at that very spot, taking advantage of the man being distracted by Kenny, who was still laughing and jumping with a crazed expression. Poor guy. The battle had pushed him over the edge. I just hoped I was going to be able to pull him back.

I pushed my mental trigger. Bright light shot from my hand, once again hurting enough that I couldn't suppress a groan. It hit the man just where I'd aimed, and he staggered back, a look of surprise plastered all over his scared face. His wings drooped before he fell, landing on his back with a crack. I ran over, made sure he was dead, before returning to Clay and Peter.

Clay was unconscious again, and Peter looked grim. His hands were drenched in blood, still pressing on Clay's chest wound.

"That's three," he said grimly. "One to go, unless Kenny killed her. I really have no idea."

"Kenny," I shouted. "Come here."

He'd started dancing around the man's body, jumping on the wings. When he heard me, he looked at me, his grin too wide, his eyes too bright. "You killed an angel. You're going to burn in Hell."

He cackled again, and a shiver ran down my back. The

Kenny I knew was gone. He started shooting bright lights into the sky, aimlessly pointing left and right.

It was only a matter of time until he hit one of us by accident.

"We need to stop him," Peter muttered, voicing my thoughts.

"There's no way we can get close," I whispered back. "Can we knock him out somehow? Can our tech do that? I don't want him to get hurt."

Peter nodded. "I can. Put your hands on mine and take over for a second. We need to keep pressure on Clay's wound."

I did as instructed, and as soon as Peter was sure that I knew what I was doing, he turned to Kenny. My crazy guy was doing something that looked like a strange tribal dance while still shooting all over the place. Yup. Crazed as fuck.

"I hope this works," Peter muttered under his breath and pointed at Kenny. A red lightning bolt shot out, hitting Kenny in the head. He looked at us for a moment, the craziness draining from his expression, before slowly crumbling into a heap.

Peter ran to him and put two fingers on his throat. "He's fine, just unconscious."

Thank goodness. That left Peter and me as the only ones awake. Hopefully, Blake was still in the tree, safe from the fighting.

No. He wasn't. There he was, stumbling toward us, visibly having trouble staying upright.

"I killed a woman," he shouted. "I'm a killer."

He collapsed. I wanted to run to him, but I had to stay with Clay and keep pressure on his wound. Peter was already racing to his brother, though.

That was three of us down. Two conscious.

Even though we'd killed our enemies, there was no way we'd survive like this. I could feel the life draining out of Clay. Kenny would wake up again, but who knew what state his mind would be in. And Blake...

We were so screwed.

[15]

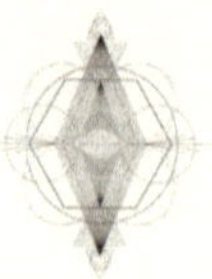

"Can you hear me?" Tim yelled in my ear. "Damn it, this thing should be working now."

"Tim?" I never thought I'd be so happy to hear from him. "Tim, we're in trouble."

He laughed. "To say the least. Yes, you are in trouble. Blake and Clay. You need to get them help, too, and some of Kenny's tech is short circuiting his brain. Has been going on, I think, for a while. I've got everyone's read outs. Don't ask me how I did it, because... it's complicated. Look, I'm going to save you. All of you. What can I say? We still want to believe in happy endings."

Sometime, I was going to ask him who *we* was. Right then, I couldn't have cared less.

"I am about to do something... potentially very bad for me, but hopefully, I can get away with it. This is important. The lights are going to be shut off. They are going to stay like that for five minutes. In that time, I want you to not move. And I mean not an inch. Just a breath. Stay where you are. When you feel like you're falling, don't fight it."

I had a second to look up at Peter. He was the only one

here going anywhere potentially. "When the lights go off, let yourself fall and don't move. Or rather the opposite order."

He stared at me, his mouth open. "What?"

The lights went out, and a siren sounded. I had enough time to gasp.

And then, I was falling.

I MUST HAVE PASSED OUT. When I woke up, I was somewhere else.

"Eileen, I need you to get up." It was Tim's voice. "Eileen, wake up now."

I looked around. Where in the hell was I? Some kind of ship? It jarred left and right. "Tim?"

"Good. Okay. Listen, Peter will be up soon. This is important. You are about to lose my signal. You won't get it back again. The next time you see us, you'll really be seeing us. You are on a spacecraft. It is taking you to where I live when I'm not there with you. The thing is, where I'm from, it's a slave planet. When you get here, they will assume that you are just more slaves they are sending to work here. We will have to deal with that when you arrive. I'm not even sure yet. One problem at a time. For now, you need to get Blake and Clay healed and the faulty tech out of Kenny. This whole ship is automated. There are medical robots. Turn them on." Something scratchy came through the line. "And dye your hair. All of you. The trip will be about a month. It's a sucky trip. We're on another ship a little ahead of you. Don't forget to dye your hair. All females have to be bleached blonde, or the aliens kill them. There's dye in the bathroom. Good luck, Eileen. I'll see you soon."

Just like that... he was gone.

I couldn't think. What had happened? I looked left and right. Okay. He'd given me instructions. Turn on the medical robots. I ran over to them, recognizing them from when we'd managed to escape into the tunnels. They looked the same. I hit the button on three of them, and red lights signaled they were on. Zapping noises started as they scanned the room. Yes, I had bruises and pain, but I wasn't the issue.

"Them." I pointed at my friends who were all strewn around the floor.

Peter lifted his head. "What the hell?"

I rushed over to him. "Peter? You okay?"

The robots moved fast. There must be some kind of signal that indicated who was the most hurt. They went to Clay and Blake, one finally going to Kenny. Would it know his tech was damaged? If the aliens could do this, why didn't they? I knew that answer. They didn't care if we died.

"What's happening?"

I shook my head. "We're on a spaceship heading to a slave planet."

He looked around, finding Blake, relief spreading across his face. He nodded, like that answered his question, and hauled himself off the floor. Limping, but not seeming to be otherwise hurt, he made it to the window. "Fuck. We are."

I hadn't considered looking out into space, but now I needed to see, too.

Even knowing what I'd see, it still stole my breath. Down below, growing distant by the second, was our home planet. Earth. I touched the side of the window like it might let me feel the planet below. She really was *blue*.

My tears surprised me, and I wiped them away, looking

at Peter. He seemed lost in his own thoughts, and I left him to them. I didn't want to watch Earth vanishing.

Instead, I looked around. We were in the main room of a ship. The room next door was a control room that presumably was auto-piloting us to our next destination.

I didn't know how to fly a ship, and I had no idea where I'd send us if I did. The robots working on my guys beeped and rolled around, holding needles and scalpels. I quickly looked away. I wasn't going to watch that either.

I hoped they'd be okay.

There was a galley with food and three bedrooms. Each bedroom had a small bathroom attached. This ship was practically heaven. Could I just stay here? I stumbled into the bathroom and practically threw myself under the spray of a hot shower.

That was when the tears really hit me. What had happened? All the things we'd done, all the hell we'd been through, the lives I'd taken.

Time was so skewed there, I didn't even know how long I'd been in there.

The shower curtain pulled back, and Peter was suddenly there. He threw his clothes aside, and his arms came around me, holding me against him.

"You're okay. You are. My girl. We got away. I don't know what's going to happen next, but you're okay."

I wasn't, and he knew it. But Peter was also not okay. None of us were or ever would be. Still, for a second under the hot water, I decided to pretend he could possibly be telling me the truth. Or maybe it was simply that in that moment, I actually was. We lived second by second. In this particular spot in time, we were okay.

We stayed just like that for what seemed like forever. Eventually, I pulled back. There was shampoo and soap. I smiled at him while I washed his hair. This was what normal couples did. They took care of each other.

He spun me around, washing me as I had him.

This should be a sexy moment, but I could see in his gaze what I knew had to be in mine, exhaustion.

Eventually, he shut off the water, and we wrapped each other up in towels.

"I checked on the others before I came in. They're all in serious condition, but the robots have stabilized each of them to the point of being out of danger. Not critical. No estimation yet on any of their time frame to recovery."

I nodded. Maybe the basic function of speech had left me. We walked together, climbing into the bed. It fit us both, but barely. I wasn't not sure what happened after that.

My eyes... they just didn't want to stay open.

I WOKE UP LATER. It was dark in the room, and Peter slept half on top of me like he would block the world from getting to me with his body. My brain was back on, the survival mode I'd been in earlier was gone.

I ran my fingers over the muscles on Peter's back. My breasts ached, and my insides were hot. I wanted him. We'd both been nearly killed. A lot. If he were awake, he'd tell me not to overthink it.

I kissed his neck, and he didn't stir. Moving slightly, I kissed him again, this time on his shoulder, then his chin. Part of him woke up. Against my leg, his cock stirred to life. His eyes opened slowly, and he smiled down at me.

"Nice way to wake up."

How I loved his accent.

I kissed his lips hard, making my intentions known. This was not meant to be simply an early morning wake up kiss. I wanted the man. I wanted him in every way possible right then.

He got the picture fast. Pulling me under him fully, Peter kissed me as though his life depended on it, like I was oxygen, and he needed me to breathe.

Peter grabbed onto my hands, pinning them above my head. I moaned. Yes, that was what I wanted, to not think. I'd chosen this, initiated it. I wasn't going to live long enough to have to worry about any consequences of doing this. At this point, he could be in charge. *Make all the choices, please. Take control.*

His kisses were scorching, demanding. There was fire between us. It might burn, but that was fine. We rubbed against each other with no finesse. It was part dry humping, part desperation to feel anything at all.

"Eileen," he said against my mouth. "I fucking love you."

I nodded. "Me, too. You."

Peter sighed against my neck. "Good."

How could I not love him? We'd been in hell together and come out the other side. Our story was screwed up, and so were the truths of our feelings going to be. He let go of my wrist, but I didn't move my hands. He'd put them there, and he hadn't yet told me to move them.

Peter kissed the length of my body. I squirmed. I needed... I needed... oh fuck, I just needed.

When he got to my legs, he spread them apart with a strong push. I moaned. He hadn't touched me there yet, but it felt like he had. Even his eyes were a stroke, and he looked at me everywhere.

With a smile that could only be called predatory, Peter

kissed my pussy. I cried out, and he lifted his gaze to mine. "You're so wet."

"Dripping for you." I didn't even know where those words came from. I didn't talk like this, not ever.

Peter dropped his head again, this time finding my clit with his tongue. With a long stroke, he pressed against the bundle of nerves. I jolted, and he put his hand on my thighs to stop me from moving. That proved futile. I was very soon grinding against his tongue. Completion was close, but I couldn't get there. What he did felt incredible, but it wasn't enough, not nearly. I wasn't going to get there like this.

"Peter," I could hear the beg in my voice. "Please. Inside of me."

He scooted up. "That's what you want? My cock? You want to feel me fucking you?"

"Please," I begged again.

"Yes." He took my nipple in his mouth. "In a minute."

I groaned. This was the sweetest torture.

"Good girl. Wait for it. I've dreamed of this. In that hellhole, I dreamed of being with you like this."

I couldn't think. Every moment felt like an hour, and yet I never wanted it to end. Finally, and too soon, he pressed himself inside of me. I stretched to fit him, my muscles clenching around him when he finally got himself balls deep.

His hand smoothed the hair off my forehead. "I love how you've stayed like that, your hands over your head where I put them, like my good girl." He kissed my nose. Soon he would move, soon he had to. "Touch me now, would you?"

The pleading gaze he gave me almost undid me. Yes, Peter needed my touch as much as I did his. I hooked my legs around his waist so I could take him even deeper. At the same time, I wrapped my arms around him.

He jerked inside of me. In and out, slow, and then fast. Every pass ground his pelvis to my clit, and I cried out. Pleasure was pain. The build up from before returned swiftly, and I knew it wouldn't be long until I'd be where I needed to be. We cried out together, our moans the only sound other than the engines around us.

"Take it." He kissed my lips over and over. "Take what you need. Give it to me."

I did. I shattered into a million pieces. My orgasm came in an explosion. I didn't just come, I fell apart, tears streaming down my face before I bit down on his shoulder. So many needs, so many desires, all of it Peter's. He thrusted into me. Once, then twice, before he emptied himself deep inside of me. Whatever my earlier reservations had been, I didn't care anymore. They'd probably made me infertile anyway. And I wasn't living long enough for anything to matter. I didn't care right now. I'd rationalize later when I wasn't so fucking happy.

I kissed his face while I tried to calm down. His eyes were closed while he held himself over me. Little jerks rocked both of us on and off.

Eventually, he opened his eyes to stare at me. "You're so beautiful."

I kissed him, softly. "Peter." I didn't know why I said his name. I just needed to.

He wrapped us both up in the blanket and rolled off of me but only to drag me to his side. "It's still early." Peter nodded toward the clock. I hadn't even noticed it. "And we have nowhere to go anyway. Go back to sleep, Eileen."

I nodded. That sounded like a great idea.

I woke up to a beeping noise in the other room. Peter snored, and I wasn't going to bother him about it. He wouldn't know how to fix something being off any more than I would. I grabbed my clothes and decided against them. Instead, I checked the closet and put on a jumpsuit I found. It was blue and shapeless, but not too long, and I made my way out of the bedroom.

Clay was awake. Well, sort of. He sat up, his head in his hands. I walked over to him, placing my hand on his back. "Hey, Clay."

He stared at me a long second. "What's..."

His voice trailed off. I walked past him to the read-out the medical robot had left. The recommendation was sleep and pain pills. Did we have those? It seemed we did, as there was a pile of them next to Clay.

"Okay." I put my arm around him. "Lean on me. You're going back to bed."

"Eileen." He said my name slowly. "Okay?"

I kissed his cheek. "Yes. Thanks to you. I'm okay. We're all going to be okay."

Blake and Kenny were still being worked on. I couldn't watch.

Instead, I helped Clay walk toward the bedroom after I grabbed the pills. Laying him down on the second bed in the room where Peter still slept, I helped him into the bed. Running to the bathroom, I grabbed some water and got Clay to swallow them before he passed out. His color was good. Maybe we'd be okay.

I sat there for a second between the beds where two of my guys slept and tried to breathe. Panic was my middle name right now, but we had a month to deal with it, and I'd just have to take this one day at a time.

Peter rolled over, touching my shoulder. "He's going to be fine now."

I looked over at him. Images from what we'd done in the middle of the night flooded me, my cheeks heating up. "Can we do that again, soon?"

His smile was huge. "Fuck, yes. I... I meant what I said. I love you."

"I meant it, too."

Next to me, Clay started to snore. I smiled. This was going to be our normal for a while.

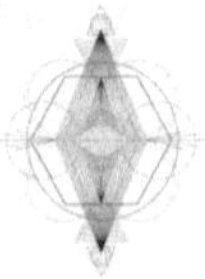

It was a very strange feeling to be on a spaceship. Not just because we were in the middle of nowhere, with Earth far away, but because there was nobody threatening us. It was just the five of us. No enemies, no aliens.

While the others were slowly recovering, Peter and I explored the ship. It wasn't very big, but sufficient for us. Everything was automated, from the navigation to the cleaning. Little bots whizzed around the rooms, wiping any speck of dust and dirt that they could find.

We didn't even have to cook for ourselves. Two vending machines in the galley offered several different food options. Nothing special, not much taste, but it was more food than I'd had in weeks, months even. If I got hungry, I'd simply go and press a button, and have a full plate. It was heaven, really.

But my favorite part of the ship was the second shower, not the one Peter and I had used on our first day. It didn't use running water as I'd expected, but hot steam that seemed to seep into my skin and make me feel squeaky clean. The guys preferred the traditional shower, but that was fine by me. I'd claimed this one, and nobody was going to take it from me.

"Hey."

Clay took a seat by my side. I was on the observation deck, a small room next to the bridge. A whole wall was taken up by a massive window offering a view of dark, endless space. I stayed here a lot, sitting on some pillows I'd thrown on the floor. The vastness of the universe made me feel free. Insignificant, yes, but free. With so many planets and stars, why would anyone come after someone so tiny like me? We weren't interesting. We might be finally safe, at least for a while.

"Hey."

His body touched mine, warm and comfy. He was the tallest of the guys and just the right height for me to lay my head on his shoulder. He wrapped an arm around my lower back and pulled me closer.

"You like this place, don't you?"

"Mhmm." I snuggled against him, soaking in his warmth. He smelled of home. So perfect.

"I still can't believe we're in space. I mean, look at it. So many stars. So many civilizations out there, and we have no idea how many. I'd love to go and explore."

I blinked up at him. "You would?"

"Earth is broken. People there just survive, but I doubt we'll ever thrive again. It's time to find a new home for us. Somewhere beautiful." He pointed at a bright star to our right. "That one. For all we know, it could be habitable. We could fly there and build a new life. Be happy. Live together."

"That would be lovely," I whispered. "A new life."

"Nobody would find us. Nobody would tell us what to do. No more lies, no more deaths. Just... a home."

Tears pricked my eyes. His words came from somewhere deep, somewhere precious. I wanted him to be right. That we could just choose a planet and settle there. That we'd be safe. But I knew it wouldn't be that easy. The ship was on autopilot, and while I'd tried to find a way to change it to manual controls, I'd failed. So had Peter. I wasn't sure if Clay had tried yet. It was his first day out of bed.

We sat in silence, looking out into space. It was beautiful.

※

KENNY WAS the only one who'd not woken up yet. Blake still had a slight fever and was in bed, but he was no longer delirious, and the meds the robots were giving him seemed to work. He kept wanting to get up, but I'd threatened to never kiss him again if he left his bed before the robots said he could.

Clay had a nasty wound on his chest, but it was healing well. He was pretty proud of it. His battle scar, he called it. I really didn't want to be reminded of that battle, though. All the people I'd killed. All those unnecessary deaths.

I dreamed of their faces every night. I couldn't remember much of the dreams, just fuzzy memories, but I woke up drenched in sweat. I wasn't sure if the guys had similar nightmares, but if they did, they kept quiet about it.

I stroked back a lock of Kenny's hair from his forehead. His face was scrunched up in a grimace, as if he was having a bad dream he couldn't escape. He'd been unconscious ever since we'd woken up on board the ship. Tim had told me to get the faulty tech out of Kenny's body, but I didn't know what to do and neither did the robots. They'd stabilized him, tended to the wounds he'd had, but he didn't wake up. Something was wrong with him, and it tore my heart to pieces watching him like that. I had no idea how to help him. I felt so powerless that I wanted to throw things at the wall and break a robot or two. I needed Tim to tell me what to do, but he'd been quiet ever since that last message. If he'd told the truth, I wouldn't hear from him until we landed on the slave planet. I kind of missed him. His voice. The way he looked after me. Guided me. I hated him at the same time. He was taking us to a slave planet where goodness knew what was going to happen to us. Why on Earth would he even do that? He'd kept saying that he wanted to keep me safe, but being turned into a slave was kind of the opposite of safe.

At least I'd found the hair dye he'd mentioned. I wasn't going to use it until we approached the planet, but it was good to know that I wasn't going to be killed on sight for not having blonde hair. What a weird rule that was.

Clay stood behind me. "If Tim told you to get the tech out of him, that means he thinks you can."

I sighed. "Maybe he vastly overestimated my ability to do things."

Peter entered the room, barefoot and shirtless. The sight distracted me for half a second. Now that we'd made love—and I couldn't believe that was the phrase I used to think about it but, there it was—it was like we couldn't stop. It was Peter who woke me from my nightmares, showing me night after night with his body that I was safe and with him. Clay was up now, and some of that might change.

The dynamics of this were going to have to work themselves out.

"What's going on?"

Clay smirked at him. "Did your shirt fall off?"

He rolled his eyes. "I just woke up."

I didn't blame him for sleeping in. Getting up with me night after night had to be exhausting. "Clay and I were talking about the tech problem. I don't know how to fix Kenny."

Clay put his hand on the small of my back and stepped forward until we were side by side. "And what I was going to say was that maybe you do."

"I'd know if I did." Wouldn't I? "What do you mean?"

"Maybe your tech can remove his tech."

We'd been living like we were normal humans since we'd gotten on this ship. But Clay wasn't wrong. I had an incredible amount of stuff in me that I didn't know how to use. No one had given me instructions, and outside of fighting and killing, I wasn't sure I knew how to do anything at all.

"He's right," Peter nodded. "When I need to enact an ability and at this point, I know how to do it because I've been at it longer I think about it really hard, and the tech appears. We do it while fighting without thinking about it."

I stared at Kenny. Okay... technology inside of me... I need to fix tech in someone else. My hand changed, a glove appearing over it, burning me as it did. My other fingers suddenly had scalpels on the nails. What the hell?

I gasped.

"Easy," Clay whispered in my ear. "You're always a miracle, Eileen. You got this."

I swallowed. Maybe I did, and maybe I didn't. If the way the glove pulled me toward Kenny was any indication, I was going to be cutting him open and pulling something out of the side of his neck.

"Have I mentioned how bad I am with medical procedures? I couldn't even watch you when you were getting fixed, Clay."

He laughed. "Well, I'll catch you if you faint."

Great.

I really didn't want to watch as my hands made the first cut. Blood welled from the wound, from an injury I'd inflicted. I hated myself at that moment. Luckily, Kenny was unconscious. Hopefully, he didn't somehow feel pain.

My hands moved without my doing. I was a passenger in my own body, helplessly watching. The fingers of my gloved right hand spread open the wound while the left lengthened the cut. A trickle of blood ran down Kenny's neck and onto the mattress, but my tech seemed to be able to see what it was doing nonetheless. Once the wound was big enough, the scalpel changed shape. Yes, the metal was actually transforming as if it were putty. It now looked like the end of a screwdriver. That definitely wasn't metal found on Earth.

I suppressed a squeal as my hand plunged the screwdriver into the wound, hitting something hard. Hopefully tech, and not Kenny's spinal cord. I looked at Clay, feeling both helpless and clueless.

"Your tech knows what it's doing," he said calmly. "Trust it."

"You talk as if it's sentient."

He chuckled. "Not sentient, but intelligent. There's some sort of AI that's wired to our brains. It's how it knows when it's needed. My theory until now was that it's activated by adrenaline, but that can't be true for you. You weren't in an emergency situation, yet your tech is fixing Kenny. Maybe yours is different from ours. More advanced. More intelligent."

A searing pain shot through my left index finger, but it was pressed into the wound, and I couldn't see what was happening. It was probably changing into yet another instrument. This was so creepy.

Suddenly, Kenny groaned. Fuck. He was waking up while I was operating on him.

"Peter, hold him in case he starts to move. Clay, stand over there so he can see you if he opens his eyes. I don't want him to panic."

They did what I'd asked without question. I missed Clay's touch already, but now Peter was close to me, not quite touching but enough for me to breathe in his scent.

I willed my tech to be faster. I needed to finish this before Kenny woke up. My hands hurt, the same burning sensation I always got when the tech burst from my skin. I didn't care though, as long as it was fixing Kenny.

He moaned again.

"It'll be over soon," I whispered, hoping I was right. "Just sleep."

My left fingers resurfaced, drenched in blood. The screwdriver had disappeared, giving way to a strange tool with two small prongs. My right hand stopped holding the wound open, and instead, pressed Kenny's skin together. It seemed I was done repairing Kenny's tech. The prongs lined up along the wound's edges, then something metal shot out, almost like a stapler. Bit by bit, it sewed together Kenny's skin until nothing remained but a neat, metal-lined scar.

My hands went floppy for a moment before I had control again. I stared at my bloody fingers, now all human again. Spots flashed before my eyes, and then my stomach lurched.

I ran for the bathroom, emptying the contents of my

stomach into the toilet. Oh yeah... I never, never, ever wanted to do that again. Gross. Yuck. Blah.

I turned around to find Clay stood there holding a glass of water. "So, you're not a... medical sort of a person. You do everything else with such ease. We all have our things."

I got up, looking for the toothbrush I'd deemed my own, and quickly cleaned up. Clay waited for me by the bathroom door.

"Did Kenny wake up?" I asked when I was done.

"Nope. And the medical robots are all over him now. That done, they seem to be acting like they can fix him."

That was good news. I hoped.

"What should we do?"

Clay shrugged. "Now, or when we get to this slave planet?"

"Now. I can't think about the slave planet. That's too much."

He took my hand in his, bringing it to his mouth. "Let's see what we can learn about the aliens from being on this ship."

"Good call." I blinked. "How do we do that?"

He led me to the communal area and pointed at a screen. "Their entertainment."

Clay walked over and turned it on. The screen changed for a second, followed by video footage of the arena where we'd been. My mouth fell open. I didn't speak alien, but it was clear it was some kind of news report. They were all pointing at a big giant hole in the ground. I chewed on my lip. Was that how we'd gotten out?

Pulling my gaze from that, I stared at the aliens talking. We'd all seen them when they took over Earth. They looked like giant cockroaches covered in black hair with pointy hands. They clicked when they talked. Monsters, my father had called them.

Maybe they were. But they were technologically advanced monsters, and they had beaten us in days.

We'd had no defenses. How many planets had they done that to? Tim's for sure. How many stars out there in the black distance had fallen that fast? Had anyone survived them?

Did anyone manage to fight back and win?

Or did they only pick planets they knew they could overthrow and enslave the population?

I stared at the scene on the screen some more.

"Penny for your thoughts." Clay wrapped his arms around me from behind.

"I'm not sure there are pennies anymore." Money stopped having meaning five years earlier.

He laughed gently. "But the expression holds."

"Hey," Peter called over to us. "I'm going to go talk to Blake. See if he's coherent. Have fun with your alien news."

I leaned on Clay. He was big, strong, and gentle with me. "Does anyone beat them? That's what I wanted to know."

"How would we find out?" Clay sighed. "But I'd like to. I'd blow them up. Bit by bit."

We sat down on the floor together to stare more at the news. I couldn't understand the language, but I got the gist. They didn't know what had happened in their tech arena. Maybe they thought we were all dead in that hole. I hoped that's what they thought.

Minutes passed. This wasn't going to get us as far as I'd hoped.

I couldn't even figure out if this was a broadcast by the cockroach aliens or by others, maybe the ones who'd built this ship. With the way it was laid out, from the furniture to the cutlery, it seemed made for humanoids.

Clay switched off the screen, and we sat in silence. I liked that about Clay. I could be silent with him without it feeling uncomfortable.

"So, you and Peter," he said after a while. "Is it serious, or an end-of-the-world kind of thing?"

I'd been waiting for this conversation to happen, and yet, I'd been dreading it. Relationships weren't something I was familiar with, and having four people squashed into my little heart... I wasn't sure this could have a happy ending.

"Do you love him?" he asked when I didn't reply.

"Yes." I didn't hesitate. It wasn't something I was ashamed of. I wasn't going to change my feelings, no matter what the world threw at me.

"We kissed."

I nodded. Yes, we had. And it had been amazing. Down there, beneath the forest. Waking up to his kiss had been one of the best moments of my life.

"Was that our last kiss?" He sounded unsure. "Did you choose Peter?"

I turned to him and looked him straight in the eye. "Yes. I chose him." His expression shattered, and he looked to the floor, but I put my hand on his cheek and forced him to look at me. "But I'm not done choosing. Nobody is going to tell me who to love. Not the aliens, not human convention, nobody. I love him. I also love other people."

I could almost see the spark of hope lighting in his blue eyes. "You do?" he whispered.

"If they love me back. I wouldn't force my love onto anyone. I'm not that greedy."

A smile curved his beautiful lips. "Want to give me an example?"

"Of what?"

"Of who else you love." His smile turned cheeky. Gone was his self-doubt. He'd already found his answer.

I pulled him closer, my fingers tangling in his curls until our lips were a breath apart. I fought the urge to kiss him just long enough to say that one word he was waiting for. "You."

[17]

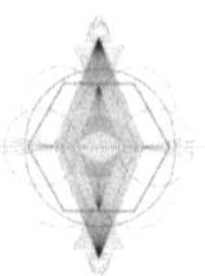

Nostrils flared, he let out a harsh breath. "I want to make love to you, Eileen. I want that more than anything. And if I haven't lost my chance to love you, then I would ask you to put me on the list in your heart. I'll happily share. You said it down in the arena, we only have moments. That hasn't changed. Please love me, too."

I said it again. "I do."

He nodded. "Just needed to hear it. Again. Maybe again." His smile was huge. "That place we were... by the giant window. Come there with me."

I let him lead me along, his hand hugging mine. "You like it here, too?"

"I do." He kissed my neck, running his hands over my back. "And I want to make love to you right here, right now. With the endless possibilities of space here with us."

I wasn't a romantic. Not really. Clay clearly was, and in that moment, I loved every word he said to me. I kissed his chin, then moved over to kiss both of his cheeks. Taking a step back, I pulled my shirt off before I set it aside. "Right here?"

His eyes were huge, and he swallowed. "Yes."

"Great." I threw myself at him, and he caught me. Clay was strong. I loved that about him. We kissed like we battled, perfectly in rhythm with one another. He touched my breasts. There were no bras on this ship, and I was bare under my clothes. He must have liked it, because he moaned as he squeezed them. I held on, kissing him everywhere I could find.

Heat traveled through my body. I loved the noises he made. Squirming to get closer, I clung to his body. "Why do you have so many clothes on, and I'm here, naked?"

Clay snorted. "Well, you did strip. Fast. Gotta give a guy a chance to catch up."

He stepped back from me to pull off his shirt and remove his pants. I guessed both of us had to go without underwear this month.

I stared at Clay for a long moment. He was strong and brutally scarred. I ran my fingers over his abs, touching a mark wherever I found them. "I bet these all have stories."

"I'm sure they do, but I can't remember them anymore. Everything before you has become a blur. Order me what to do, Eileen. Tell me what you want. Fuck, if you want to, instruct me to beg. I will do whatever. I am yours."

I cupped his cheek. "I don't want that from you. I just want whatever time we can have together. I want it to be real. I want it to be ours."

"It is." He kissed one cheek and then the other.

I decided right then I needed to forget. Clay wanted me to have what I needed. Well, this was what I needed.

I reached between us, stroking his cock. It must have taken him by surprise. He startled before he threw his head back and moaned, loud and unashamed.

His sounds made heat pool between my legs, almost

as if he'd touched me already. I slid my hand along his length, savoring his expression as his pupils dilated and his lips opened to breathless gasps. I didn't quite know what I was doing, but his beautiful moans were a good indication of what was working. I loved the power I felt as I stroked him. I was in charge. Finally, I could decide what to do. I was in control of both Clay and myself. No aliens.

"That feels so good." Clay groaned. His hands were on his hips; the only place we touched were my hands on his cock. Yet, it felt as if our bodies were pressed against each other already. I was trembling with need, but I wanted to delay the inevitable further. I didn't want it to be over too quickly. The space outside was eternal. Why shouldn't this moment also last forever?

He jerked in my hand, and he stepped back, breathing hard. "Stop. I need a moment. Shit, you almost made me come." He ran his hands through his hair, ruffling it the way I loved. He looked so sexy that way. "Now it's my turn to make you feel good. Lie down. Spread your legs."

His words made me tremble. We'd switched roles, now he was in control, but I was okay with that. No, I was fucking loving it.

The floor was cool beneath my back, but the shiver running over my skin had nothing to do with the temperature. Clay stood above me, his cock hard, his eyes fixed on my naked body. The way he looked at me made me spread my legs farther. An invitation. He took it, kneeling between my legs, running a finger over my belly. Downward, so close, and yes, I couldn't help but moan when he reached my mound. I closed my eyes and let myself fall into the sensations, bliss filling me with every stroke of his fingers. He played me like an instrument, rubbing and twirling and teasing before finally pushing into me. I jerked my hips toward him, and he chuckled.

"Patience. I've only just gotten started."

"Fuck me." I couldn't find other words than that. My body was on fire, and he was the water that could soothe the ache. I needed him.

"Not yet."

Before I could protest, he wrapped his arms around my thighs and pulled me closer. His hot breath hit my skin just before his tongue continued where his fingers had left off. He plunged into my depths, and all I could see was stars. Bright lights danced across my closed eyelids, just like the universe watching us from outside the window. I moaned and whimpered as he fucked me with his tongue. I'd never felt anything like this before. It was both gentle and wild at the same time; fulfilling, and yet, not nearly enough.

His fingernails bit into my skin as he held me tight, preventing me from closing my legs while I was squirming for more. I squeezed my breasts, craving more touch, even though all I could think about was Clay making me feel as if I was flying. My mind was a mess of scrambled thoughts and pleasure. Clay was a god of foreplay.

I finally succumbed to his ministrations, and I'd never been so happy to find pleasure in my life. I didn't think I could take one more second of his sweet torture. I called out his name, and as he pulled back, he kissed the top of my knee.

I didn't know why that sweet gesture was almost my undoing, but it loosened something inside of me that had been tight and insecure. I sucked back my tears, but failed to halt them entirely. Embarrassment flooded me.

Clay drew me to him, kissing my mouth, my cheeks. If he thought it was odd that I was crying, he didn't say a word. That was sweet of him. The man was going to undo me with his gentle kindness.

I pressed on his chest until he lay down on his back. I fitted him to me before I pushed down, taking him all the way inside of me. I was so full. For a second, I just stayed like that. We stared at each other, and I wanted to hold this memory with me forever.

I pulled up slightly before I thrust back down. Over and over. I threw my head back, pressing my fingers on my own breasts.

Clay moaned. It filled the room. I loved the sound, and I sped up my motions. He closed his eyes, his hips jerking. He must be close.

I was, too. Pleasure traveled up and down my spine, and I shook. Inside of me, Clay throbbed. With one last press, I exploded.

Colors danced in front of my eyes. Clay lost it, roaring his release. I grinned as pleasure continued to flow through me. That might have been the best sound, ever.

※

SOMETIME LATER—HOW could I even keep track of time? —I lay on top of Clay. He wasn't injured anymore at all. How and when had that happened? Did I know that? Was he totally fixed? Things were starting to blend together in my mind. I was losing details and right then, I couldn't bring myself to care. This was what happy felt like, and for now, that was more than enough. With his arms wrapped around me, I listened to his heartbeat beneath my ear. He let out a snore and turned his head before he stopped. I lifted my head. Clay had conked out pretty fast after we'd finished.

But his arms were around me as though he were awake.

Even in sleep, he didn't want me to go. I kissed his chest. How was he sleeping on the cold floor? Well, I guessed we'd all slept many places by now that weren't at all comfortable.

"Clay." I kissed him again. "You could go sleep in a bed. There are a whole lot of them."

His eyes opened slowly. "Hi."

"You're sleeping on the floor when we have beds." I repeated myself, because I was pretty sure he hadn't heard me.

"Eileen, you are lying on my chest. Wherever we are is the best place in the universe."

I nodded. "True... but you know... soft beds?"

He groaned. "We should put some mattresses in here. I want to make love to you in this room again and again while looking out to the stars."

"You're such a romantic."

"And you love it." He grinned at me, and I couldn't help it, I had to kiss him again. I could spend all day feeling his lips beneath mine. It was a soft, gentle kiss, since we were both tired, but it fit the moment. Waking up next to him was like a dream, and kissing him like this was proof that it had all been real.

A knock sounded almost at the same time as the door slid open behind us. Something snapped in me, and my mind went blank. Before I realized what was happening, I was on my feet, my arm extended toward the intruder, ready to kill if I had to.

"Hey, calm down, it's me."

I blinked, twice, until I finally processed who I was looking at. It was Peter, his hands held up, his eyes wide.

"Are you all right?" he asked softly.

Slowly, I let my arm fall to my side. My breathing was heavy, my heart beating way too fast.

"Eileen?" Clay had gotten to his feet and stood next to me, but he didn't try and touch me. He was probably scared I might attack him.

"Sorry," I muttered, lowering my gaze. Shame flashed over my cheeks.

"There's nothing to be sorry for," Peter said gently. He took a step toward me. "Is everything okay? Is your tech being weird?"

I shook my head. "No, I don't think it's the tech. Just the stress. The memories of being in Purgatory. I'm still not used to the idea that we're safe here. I keep expecting something to go wrong. Like the aliens appearing to tell us it's all just yet another game, another test. I'm not sure I would survive that without going completely crazy."

"Speaking about crazy..." Peter cleared his throat. "Kenny is awake."

I didn't hesitate. I grabbed my shirt and threw it on before I stormed past him, running through the spaceship, leaving the guys behind. It was the best excuse ever. I couldn't face them just now, not after I'd almost attacked Peter. I needed to be alone, but first, I had to check on Kenny.

He was sitting up, no longer looking as pale as he had when I'd last seen him. His eyes were free of the craziness he'd shown during the battle.

"Eileen," he greeted me with a cheery grin. "Did you bring grapes?"

I stared at him in confusion. "What?"

"An old custom. Bringing grapes to a hospital to cheer up the patients. No idea who came up with it, but I was kinda looking forward to grapes."

"I'm not sure our food machines here know what grapes are, unless there's an alien version of them. Sorry. But let's just pretend I gave you grapes, and that you're all happy now. How are you feeling?"

Kenny snickered. "You need to work on your bedside manner. But yes, I'm feeling great. Like a new man, actually. Whatever you did fixed me. And I'm not just talking about the tech that broke during the battle. I... my head is clearer. Less muddled. I think stuff was broken in there even before the battle, and you managed to heal it all."

I stared at him. "Does that mean you're no longer crazy?" Oops. I clasped my hands in front of my mouth, cursing myself for saying that.

He laughed. "Don't worry, I know I'm crazy. I don't know if I'm completely sane now, but time will tell. For now, let's assume that I'm not going to go all psycho anytime soon. Does that sound good?"

I cringed. "Yes, but please forgive me if I go psycho on you instead."

"Huh? What's wrong?"

He slid off the bed and took me into his arms before I could stop him.

"What's wrong, Brown Eyes?" he repeated.

Instead of an answer, I leaned my head against his shoulder and simply let him hold me.

He kissed the top of my head. "Do I need to kill one of them?"

"What?" I laughed. "No. You might need to kill me."

Kenny shook his head. "Not going to happen."

"Peter opened a door, and I almost attacked him. I could have killed him. I'm... out of control."

Kenny pressed his mouth to my temple, kissing me there. "Of course, you are. What's more, Peter, he gets it. He's out of control, too. We all are. They made us worse than animals, they made us monsters. It's okay. We may need to be. I mean... I'm not sure where we are, but I have a feeling we haven't been rescued to rainbows and sunshine, right?"

I smiled at him. "No, Tim did this for us. But now we're on our way to a slave planet. I have to dye my hair blonde. Bleach it. Everything could be so much worse."

He nodded. "Fun times. Then do me a favor, gorgeous, and don't lose that edge. Don't try to heal. We have to be crazy. And if that means that for now we all watch each other's backs so we don't accidentally kill each other? So be it."

I liked that Kenny always understood the harder parts of things. "I'm so glad you're not dead."

He kissed my temple again. "Me, too. I wouldn't trade this moment for anything. Now, come on. Let's go see Peter, and you can see he's fine. Is Blake okay?"

"Recovering. He's sleeping most of the day. That's normal, considering things right now, or so says the medical robots. You take it easy, too."

"We're on a spaceship, right? That's so cool. What am I going to do to overdo it?" He shrugged. "This is like a childhood dream."

We linked hands, and I brought him to the last place I'd seen Peter. He was still in the room with Clay, who was now dressed. One of them had folded my pants and put them in the corner.

"Hey." He smiled at me when I entered before nodding to Kenny. "Glad to see you're up. Come help us."

Right in front of them on the ground were pieces of technology spread all over the place. I stepped toward them. "What are you guys doing?"

Clay grinned at me. "We figure they trained us to do

certain things down in that place. So, we're going to do it. We're making weapons out of spare parts."

"Awesome." Kenny squatted down.

I was glad they were all so happy about this. A moment of joy filled me. We just needed Blake, and then it would be just like when we'd hidden away for that night. Still, the question had to be asked. "What did you take apart to do this?"

He pointed toward a metal locker in a corner of the room. "Found some weird stuff in there. I have no idea what most of those things do, but they're good for parts. I doubt any aliens will be missing them. And if they do, well, bad luck."

I sat down beside Clay and picked up a small rod with flashing lights at either side.

"Well, let's build us some toys."

[18]

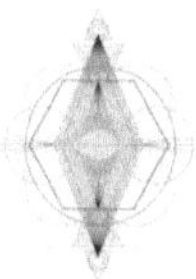

Sex was the best medicine in the world. Not just the sex, but the intimacy that came with it. The guys and I were getting closer than ever before. I could no longer imagine being without them, yet my mind refused to let me believe in a happy ending. With every hour, the spaceship carried us closer to our destination. The slave planet. Who knew what would await us there, so I tried to block it out and distract myself. Being surrounded by four gorgeous, amazing men made that very easy.

I yawned and carefully climbed over Clay. I'd been sandwiched between him and Kenny, while Peter was cuddled up at the foot end of the giant bed we'd created by placing several mattresses in the space observatory. The only one missing was Blake. The sound of him leaving the room had woken me up, but it had taken me a moment to realize.

I tiptoed away, glad the guys were deep sleepers. Peter snored softly. I'd had to push him in the ribs several times last night to get him to stop.

Blake wasn't in the galley, nor on the bridge, nor in the

small living area. The three bedrooms were empty, too, and so were the bathrooms. The ship wasn't big, so he couldn't have disappeared.

On a hunch, I walked to the loading bay, where we'd all woken up when we'd first arrived on the vessel. There he was, next to one of the medical robots.

They'd returned here after everyone had been fixed. Like silent skeletons, they stood against the wall, unmoving, only activating once we had another emergency. Yet Blake was fiddling with one of them, pressing buttons.

"I knew you'd come here," he said with a resigned sigh. He didn't turn around.

"What are you doing?"

"Do you know how to switch them on?" he asked instead of giving me an answer. The way he acted was scaring me a little.

"No, they've always done that automatically. Why, are you hurt?"

He laughed mirthlessly. "In a way. I need them to fix me. Can you help me activate one of them?"

Carefully, I put a hand on his shoulder, and he finally turned around. His eyes were lined with red, as if he'd been crying, yet there were no tears in sight. He looked as if he'd not slept at all.

"What's wrong?" I whispered, gently pulling him into my arms. He resisted a little, but then he let me hug him. He buried his face in my hair, his breath tickling my neck.

"I need to be fixed. They need to remove it."

All right, now he was really scaring me. "Remove what?"

"Whatever is linking me with my handler. I need it gone."

I gripped him tighter. "Your handler is speaking to you again?"

"Yes. And he's telling me to kill you all."

His hands wrapped around me, crushing me against him. "He keeps talking," he muttered, his voice pained. "He tells me that if I don't kill you, he's going to do horrible things to me. He's hurting me, Eileen. It hurts so fucking much."

I rubbed his back, too shocked by his words to say much. I'd thought we'd escaped our handlers. Tim wasn't able to talk to me, or so he'd said, but Blake's alien was back in the game. That meant it might be the same for the others.

"When did it start?" I asked quietly, not wanting to startle him.

"Yesterday, while I was sleeping. I thought it was a nightmare at first, but then the whisper turned into his voice, the same commanding voice I've been obeying back in Purgatory. He's back, and he's pissed. He wants me to kill you and then return the ship to him, so that he wins the game."

"The game? Didn't that stop when we left the planet as the only survivors?"

He put his hands over his ears. "I don't know, Eileen. I don't know. How do any of us know anything? Maybe Tim was just fucking with you. Maybe we're still in the game. Maybe..."

I put my hand on his forehead. He was hot again. I didn't want to freak him out. "Blake, you're not feeling well. You have a high fever again. Maybe you are hallucinating this stuff."

He pointed at the robots. "Then why aren't they coming on to fix me?"

By now he shouted. I knew that tone, I'd heard it from Kenny on the battlefield. I'd heard it a lot. Blake's tech was malfunctioning. Perhaps it was his body actually rejecting the tech. Hell, I wasn't a doctor. I didn't really know what I was talking about.

"I fixed Kenny's tech. I'll... do the same with you."

His face was pale. "Do you think you can?"

I'd hated the process the first time around, but yes, for Blake, I would do it again. I patted the table. "Lie down here."

He visibly swallowed. "Are you going to knock me out? Are we going to..."

I took a deep breath. I'd needed Clay to help me with this earlier, but he'd been up all night tinkering. I didn't want to wake Peter to see this happen to his brother. And Kenny... I didn't know if this was going to be his thing.

We did need him knocked out. "Blake, I'm going to hurt you. I'm sorry. Please forgive me. I'll hurt you, and then the robots will knock you out. Then I can fix your tech. Okay?"

He nodded, fast. "I forgive you, Eileen. I forgive you a million times over. I"

I pushed the knife out of my hand. Letting the tech jam it into Blake's shoulder. He cried out, and I winced. "Sorry. Sorry. Sorry. Sorry."

The robot turned on, and I backed off quickly. In a second, the robot had him unconscious as it repaired his arm.

"Great. Great." I was officially sweating. "Tech. On. Fix."

My body burned as it did whatever I'd asked of it. A screwdriver. A wrench. Some big red glowy thing. All of them came out of me and started to move.

Kenny's voice came over me. "Dude, what are you doing? That is very cool."

I winced. "Yeah... I did this for you, too. And I absolutely hate it. It's very yuck."

By the time I was done fixing Blake, my arms were covered in blood splatters, and sweat was pearling on my forehead. I needed a shower, and I really wanted to go back to bed. The day had only just begun, but I was exhausted already.

I let the robot clean up Blake's wound, trusting it to do a better job with sutures than my shaking hands could. My tech might have been amazing, but it was part of me and that meant it had to rely on my strength.

Kenny put an arm around my shoulders. "Let's get you cleaned up, and then I'm going to make you breakfast."

I looked at him in surprise. "You can cook?"

"No, but I can press a few buttons on the vending machines. I could probably make fried eggs, too, if you find some eggs, a cooker, and a frying pan for me."

I had to smile. "Sorry, no can do. Space food it is. I don't want to leave Blake alone. Can you watch him while I take a shower?"

Kenny stepped back and pouted. "I thought I'd accompany you to the bathroom and, you know, help you with the showering. Or I could watch, if you prefer to wash yourself." He roamed his gaze over my body. Tingles spread across my skin. He really was tempting me. Naked in his arms, safe and distracted from everything else that was going on. So tempting. But no. I had things to do, I couldn't spend yet more time having fun with one of the guys. We'd only got started on building weapons, there was a lot more to do before we were ready to arrive on the slave planet.

"Next time," I muttered. "I promise."

He grinned. "I'll be waiting in front of the bathroom every minute of the day, waiting for you." He suggestively pointed toward his crotch. "And I won't be the only one waiting."

I groaned. He could be so silly sometimes.

I left Kenny with Blake and had a quick shower, kind of regretting that I didn't take his offer. I watched as bloody water pooled around my feet. Blake's blood. I really hoped I hadn't made things worse. It had been a bit of an impulse decision, and those weren't always the best. At least if he woke up and still heard his handler talking to him, we'd know that it was real and not a tech malfunction.

I let the shower dry my hair—it made it softer than any hair dryer ever could—and headed back to the bedroom, wrapped in a towel. My clothes were there, along with two very sleepy looking men. Peter was awake, blinking at me and giving me a small wave. Clay lifted his head but continued to sleep as soon as he'd realized it was me. Lucky them. I really wanted to join them and just relax.

I took some random clothes from one of the cupboards. They weren't my size but not wide enough to get in the way.

"Where are the others?" Peter whispered.

I joined him on the bed, and he pressed a quick kiss on my cheek.

"Kiss me," I muttered, needing a lot more than just that quick peck. For some reason, I was feeling empty inside.

He cupped my face with his warm hands, and his lips met mine, kissing me ever so gently. I let myself fall against him, wrapping my arms around his back, holding on tight. I needed the closeness. The warmth. I was cold all over. The emptiness inside of me was spreading, swallowing me. Coldness poured into me as if I was stepping into a frozen lake.

Peter pulled back but kept his hands on my face. "Sweetie, what's wrong? You're shaking. Your skin is freezing."

Clay sat up with a start. "What's going on?"

"Eileen isn't well. Look, she's trembling."

He was right. My entire body was shaking with cold. My teeth chattered as icicles seemed to scrape across my skin. I moaned in pain. Something was wrong, something bad was happening to me.

I let my eyes fall shut, too exhausted to keep them open. Their voices faded, their touch was just a faint memory. I was so cold.

"Hold on."

A familiar voice inside my head. I knew him, but it was hard to think. Even my thoughts were frozen.

"Hold on."

In the here and now on the spaceship, I lifted my head. "Tim?"

"Aw... fuck me." Clay sunk back down onto the pillow. "Really?"

"Eileen? Can you hear me?"

I could. I nodded, although it was clear to me he couldn't hear me. "I can. Tim?"

"Awesome. I didn't know if I'd be able to pull this off ship-to-ship. How are you?"

He sounded downright chipper. "Well... I guess things are fine. I just had to operate on Blake's tech. I did Kenny's, too. Officially my least favorite thing to do. But we're all okay. And making do." I paused. "How close to us are you?"

"Not very. I could give you exact distances, but I think that would be confusing. Listen... there's something you should know." He cleared his throat. "I know you know me as Tim. And that's fine. I like that name. But there are two of us you've called that."

Confusion settled in my stomach, bringing with it anger and sadness. Why was nothing easy? Why was nothing as it was supposed to be? "There are two of you?"

Peter sat up, fast. "I knew it. More than one. I think there was more than one of mine, too."

"Yes. We... we're a team. I'm sorry we lied. That's how it had to be. But I'm being truthful with you now. I'm more chatty. He's more techy."

I supposed that made sense in a weird, unbelievable kind of way. Tim did seem to have a drastic change in personality. Stupidity made me feel small. At this point, I should be used to it. "How did I not know?"

"Well... how could you have?"

I leaned back against the headboard. "Does one of you hate me and one of you like me?"

He laughed, a low sound. "No, we both like you."

"Well... that's good. So, what are you reaching out about today?"

He sighed, and it moved through me. It was strange how much I'd missed hearing his voice and hadn't even known it until I heard it again. "I wanted to see if I could reach you because when you get there in two weeks, you're all going to need some guidance to get through the check in and hopefully avoid getting thrown in the Hell Pit."

The Hell Pit? "Tim..."

He interrupted. "Dye your hair if you haven't, okay? I'll talk soon. Or he will. One of us will. Talk soon."

There was static, and he was gone.

Two weeks. That was all we had until we had to leave the safety of our ship. But we were going to be ready. I put a weapon onto the stack on the floor. One down, many more to go. My tech knew what it was doing, and just like when I'd fixed Kenny and Blake, I was a passenger in my own body, watching my hands as they worked. They took scrap metal, random junk we'd found on the ship, and turned them into tools and weapons. By the time we reached our destination, we'd have an entire arsenal at our disposal.

Blake sat opposite me, silently working on something that looked like a small megaphone, but was probably a lot more lethal than that. He'd not spoken about what had happened ever since he'd woken up. I'd asked how he felt, but all he'd done was give me a small smile and a hug. Something was up with him, but he didn't seem in the mood to share. I was going to leave him to it for a while, but eventually, I'd have to make him open up. There could be no secrets between us. To survive, we had to be a team, a family. Secrets could be deadly.

Clay entered the room, sauntering over to our table that we'd turned into a workbench. He grinned at me. "How's life?"

"Busy," I said, looking up from the new tool my hands were working on. My tech had sensors that didn't need my eyes to look at what it was doing. So weird.

"Kenny is trying to reprogram the food machines to produce poison, but he says he needs silence to work. Anything for me to do here?"

I nodded toward the chair next to me. "Take a seat. Let's see what your tech can do. Where's Peter?"

"No idea, I thought he was with you."

I frowned. We were all busy preparing for the slave planet, but that left little time to spend with the guys. If I could've, I would have spent all day in bed with them, yet my mind was too rational for that. If we weren't ready in two weeks, we'd die.

Blake got up. His chair screeched over the metal floor, startling me. "I'll look for my brother."

He left without saying another word.

"What's wrong with him?" Clay asked.

I shrugged. "Not sure. He won't talk to me. I wonder if his controller really is back. He might be forbidding Blake to talk to us. If that's the case, we need to find a way to block their connection. We can't have anyone get between us, least of all those fucking aliens."

Clay grinned at me. "I love it when you swear."

I rolled my eyes. "Get busy, or I'll swear even more."

"You're so tense. What's up?"

I met his eyes and sighed. "I'm scared, okay? We don't know what awaits us. For all we know, the aliens on that planet might all have ten legs and claws. We might be the weakest of them all. I don't want to die." I pointed at him.

"And before you start with me about it, I don't want you to die either, so no big proclamations of dying for me, okay? None. We are all staying alive."

He held up his hands. "Got it. No swearing my fealty to die for you."

I snorted. "Keep that up, and I'm going to picture you wearing armor and a sword."

"If only I had one." He shook his head. "When was the last time you took a break?"

I sighed. "I don't know, actually. I've been at this all day."

"And you were up all night. Didn't think I noticed? Not that I have any idea how you sleep next to Peter with the way that he snores." He winked at me.

I rolled my eyes. "Because you never snore?"

"Fair enough. Go take a break. Go dye your hair."

I'd been putting it off. It was one of those things. Once I did it, and Tim said I had to, it meant that we really were about to land on a slave planet where all women had to have their hair bleached. I had no idea why that could be, but it was never a great thing when there were proclamations like that at all. Women all had to have bleached hair? What would they do to me if I didn't do it?

I couldn't find out right off the bat. We were being snuck onto the planet. The last thing I wanted to do was to draw attention to myself.

I got to my feet. "I'll go do it now."

"Good." He cupped my cheek before he leaned over to whisper in my ear. "Just because I don't say it doesn't mean I won't do it."

I kissed his chin. "You're very sweet to me. No one is dying."

I turned to walk away, and he called out, "I'm very

sweet to you. But don't forget I'm lethal. We're trained killers who lived through a game where everyone else died. You're a bright light in our world where we are actually very bad people."

I shook my head, calling over my shoulder. "I'm also a killer. None of us are lights."

I'd made it all the way to the bathroom, when I saw Blake standing by the window in the bedroom, staring out. He didn't turn when I entered, and I walked toward him, wrapping my arms around his waist.

He sighed, his body sagging a little bit when I held on. I'd had sex with Clay and Peter, not Blake and Kenny. That didn't mean I didn't want it.

And maybe he needed the affection as much as I did. I tugged on him. "Come with me. We can find your brother in a minute."

Blake let me lead him away from the window. "Where are we going?"

"The bathroom."

He snorted. "Together?"

"I need to dye my hair, but I thought I'd shower first. Dry my hair. And then do it. I thought maybe you might like to get naked with me in the water first." I waited. "Thoughts on that?"

He widened his eyes. "Eileen, you want that? I mean... I've been nothing but a burden."

Sometimes actions spoke more than words. As he watched, I took off my clothes, letting them pool on the ground around my feet. I was so scarred now that I hardly recognized myself when I looked in the mirror. Life had beaten the shit out of me in that game. But when Blake looked at me, his gaze heated up, and if the bulge that formed in his pants was any indication, he liked what he saw.

He stepped toward me. "Not in the shower. Can we..." His voice trailed off. "Can we make love in the bed? I want to be gentle with you. I used to be this very different person, and... I want to make love to you the way a man does when he knows he has the most precious gift imaginable in his arms."

My eyes teared up. It had to be my tech. I wasn't a woman who cried when a man told her pretty words. I turned away from him, not wanting him to see me this vulnerable. "Yes. That's good. Fine. I mean, I really want it." I was making a mess of this. "Let's do it."

"Are you sure? You can take that shower first. I can help you with your hair. I don't want you to put everything aside just because I want to be with you."

"I want to be with you, too," I whispered, my voice choking up. "Fuck everything else. Just take me to your room and make love to me."

He smiled, not just with his lips, but his eyes, too. "That can be arranged."

He picked me up as if I weighed nothing and carried me in his arms, pressing me against his chest. We ended up in the closest bedroom, and as soon as the door closed behind us, his lips were on mine, warm and hungry. He sat me on the bed, our mouths never parting, and gently let his hands roam across my back. His tongue danced with mine to music only we could hear. I cupped his face, pulling him closer, not wanting him to leave me. I craved him so much that it physically hurt. I needed him.

Blake gently pushed me backward until I lay on the bed with him on top of me. His legs straddled mine, his chest hovered above me, just close enough to stroke against my breasts. My nipples were hard, and with every accidental touch, sparks raced across my skin and right into my core. Warmth and wetness were pooling between my legs, while Blake's erection was growing. He wanted to make love to me, but I wanted to have him inside me, soon. I wasn't a patient woman, and I'd been desiring him for too long.

"You taste so good," he whispered hoarsely, breaking the kiss for just a moment. "I wonder if you taste the same down there."

He sat up and pulled his shirt over his head. Scars lined his chest, yet there was no hiding his chiseled abs. Two weeks of having as much food as we wanted had made all of us less starved, and in Blake's case, even more beautiful. I didn't care about the scars. I had them, too. Scars were a sign that we'd survived and triumphed over adversity. We'd fought and won, and we'd do the same thing again and again until we were free.

"Take off your pants."

He helped me out of them then spread my legs. Cool air touched my core, and I sucked in a breath. He'd barely touched me, yet I was ready to be taken by him. Or made love to, in his words.

Blake put his hands on my thighs and gently parted them some more.

"Beautiful," he whispered. "I don't think I've ever seen something so exquisite."

He pressed a tiny kiss on my clit, barely touching my skin, yet it had me squirming against his grip. I was aching for more.

"Please," I begged, but he was already swiping his tongue over my core, making fireworks erupt inside of me. I clawed at the bed sheets, trying to keep from grinding against him, but it was only a half-hearted attempt. Why was I even holding back? There was no reason.

So I let go.

Unleashed, my body knew what it wanted, and the answer was more. I ground my hips up against his mouth, and he bit down on my clit. I cried out, gripping the bed. "Blake."

He moaned against me, his own hips pushing down on the bed when he did that. He dove his tongue deeper, leaving my clit to press inside of me, drinking me in like I was the best thing he'd ever tasted.

I squirmed beneath him. Yes, I was going to come. And it was going to be hard. Keening noises released from my throat. Noises I'd never made before.

I exploded, colors dancing in front of my eyes as tears dashed down my face. He crawled up me, raising his head to kiss them away, murmuring things I could hardly hear through the ringing in my ears. Sweet words.

"I'll always take care of you, my beautiful love."

I kissed him, pressing my tongue against his as he adjusted his body, fitting it against mine. Pulling back, I stared in his dark eyes. "Blake, do you want me to…"

He shook his head, cutting off my question. "I'm so turned on right now, you touch me, and I'll never make it inside of you."

I nodded. "I want you there."

"It's the only place I want to be."

Blake slipped inside of me. My muscles clenched around him as I got used to the feel of him. I wanted more, deeper, and he was plenty big enough to give me what I needed. I wrapped my legs around him, clasping my ankles together, but even that wasn't deep enough. No, I took my legs and placed them on his shoulders.

We both cried out.

"Eileen, how can you be like coming home?"

I didn't have the answers. I could hardly think. All I wanted was more. Oh fuck, yes, please. He pushed in me and then pulled out. We breathed hard together for a long second before he did it again.

I dug my fingers in his back as I tried to hold on for dear life. Over and over. His mouth was on mine, and as each movement drove me toward completion again, I had never tasted anything sweeter than Blake loving me. Because that was what this was. He loved me. I could feel it in every cell, every pore of my body.

The thought set me over the edge, and I came around his hard cock, milking him, drawing him deeper. His whole body jerked as he emptied inside of me.

After a moment, I drew him down so his weight covered me. I loved the pressure of it, loved being able to hear him breathe heavily, loved the vibrations of his body on top of mine. Kissing his shoulder, I closed my eyes. I would be perfectly fine with falling asleep right here.

He lifted his head and kissed my closed eyelids. With a smile on my face and in my heart, I opened them. "Hi."

"Hi." He stared at me for a long moment. "You keep having to save me. I promise that I will stop being something else you have to take care of. I'm strong, and you are my priority."

I ran my hands through his hair. "Blake... are we alone right now?"

He scrunched down his eyebrows. "Who else would be in here with us?"

"Are you still hearing your handler? And don't run

away because I'm asking you questions. This is you and me, okay? You're mine. What we just did? It's... binding for me. I'm not able to explain it, and I realize I make no sense. I'm sleeping with all of you." Well, almost all of them. I hadn't with Kenny yet, but no question, that was coming. "I attach with affection like this. I just do. Unless you tell me to go away, I'm going to want to keep you forever. Fuck, I am rambling." And crying apparently, as I wiped at my cheeks. "This is my heart speaking to your heart. What is going on with you?"

"Are you sure you want to know?" he asked, his words almost lost under his breath. I wasn't sure if he wanted to talk about it, but I needed to hear it.

"Yes. Tell me, please."

He sighed deeply. "You didn't manage to fix me. You only made me realize that I'm far more broken than I thought. We always assumed Kenny was the crazy one, but actually, it's me."

He tried to turn away but I clutched his arms, refusing to let go. "What do you mean?"

"I can still hear the voice, but it's no longer that of my handler. I think it's in my head, Eileen. You fixed the tech, but the voice is still in there, talking to me, telling me what to do. I'm crazy. Hearing voices, that's as crazy as it goes. What if it never really was my handler who talked to me? What if I just imagined it all? Killed those people because I wanted to, and not because I was forced?"

My heart beat faster at his revelations. Hearing voices wasn't a good sign.

"Could it be a new handler?" I asked carefully.

He blinked, tears pooling in his eyes. I wanted to reach out and wipe them away, but I somehow knew that if I moved, if I touched him that intimately, he would bolt. I had one chance to find out what was going on, and I had to do it now.

"Unless he's invaded my brain and sucked out every single bad memory, then no. He knows everything about me. He tells me of all the horrible things I've done, and then he orders me to do something even worse. I fight him, trust me, I do, but it's so hard. I'm exhausted, Eileen, and that's with us being on a ship without doing anything. Once we're on the planet and have threats from the outside again... I'm not sure I'm going to be able to make it."

A tear dropped onto my cheek. His, not mine, although I was having a hard time holding my own tears back. He looked so lost. I wanted to tether him, be his anchor in the depths of his despair, but I knew he was going to push me away if I offered to help. I would probably do the same in his situation. I wasn't used to accepting help, and neither was he. We were so similar in that regards. Two lost souls, broken, untethered.

I opened my mouth to say something, but he was faster.

"You can't help me, sweetheart. I'm too far gone. I know you want to fix me, but there's nothing to fix. My tech is working. It's my mind that's crazy. Unless you find some antipsychotics or whatever, I'm not going to get better."

I looked at him, almost glaring. I needed him to understand I was serious. "You don't get to say that. You don't get to give up. We'll find a way. I promise."

He laughed harshly. "Has nobody ever told you not to lie?"

"I'm not lying. I'm making a promise, and I keep my promises. You're going to get better, Blake. And I swear, if you give up, if you listen to the voice, I'm going to make you pay for that."

He raised an eyebrow. "Making threats?"

I nodded grimly. "And if I have to, I'll tie you to the bed and spank you."

Laughter echoed in my head. "I didn't think you were into that," Tim's voice sounded, accompanied by an agonizing headache.

"Tim," I groaned, before everything went black.

"Eileen." Blake's voice. Loud. Insistent. I wanted to respond to it, but I couldn't. Not right then.

"Sorry about this."

I looked around. I was in a gray room. I stood, alone, looking around at nothing to see. Just Tim's voice speaking to me.

"Where am I?"

He sighed. "I'm uploading some programming you're going to need to get through the next stop. Once you get there, you're going to be separated from the others. I can't guarantee that, but the truth is it's pretty random who gets sent where. Whatever happens, I will find you. I will figure out how to get you where I am. Not just you, but the others, too. It's going to take some time, and you will need some skills that you would have been given if you'd won the game officially. You don't have it now. But we don't want them to realize there is anything different about any of you. When you wake up from this upload, you need to share the upload with the others. You have the tech to do that."

I sighed. It was always something. "Tim, Blake isn't okay. He's hearing voices. Not a handler."

"Yes, people come out of the games, and sometimes they're not okay." He sighed. "He'd hardly be the first person to suffer. It's awful. I know firsthand. I'll try to get to him first. Get him some help."

There was silence, and then he spoke again. "You're done. Looking forward to meeting you, sweetheart."

Sweetheart?

I sat up in bed; sweat drenched my body. All four of my guys stared at me wearing equally concerned looks on their faces, but Blake's was the worst. I hugged him to me tightly. "Nothing you did. Tim had to upload some things he needed me to have. And I need to share with all of you. Put out your wrists."

Amazing how I suddenly knew how to do this.

"Is it going to knock us out?" Kenny asked.

I shrugged. "Truthfully, I don't know."

"I'll go first." He knelt down on the bed next to me. I realized they'd put my clothes back on me, sparing me the embarrassment of doing this half-naked. "Don't let them fall on me if they knock out next."

Clay rolled his eyes. "Dude, you're not deranged anymore, but you're so not normal either."

Kenny's smile was huge. "Never was."

I touched Kenny's wrist. For a second, we stared at each other, and then a buzzing started in my fingertips. My tech was transferring to his tech. He sucked in his breath. A second later, his eyes rolled to the back of his head, and I caught him while he fell forward.

"Guess that answers that question." Blake shook his head.

I stared at his defeated gaze. "Tim is going to help you.

Okay? I need you to hold on to that thought. When you're all up again, I'll explain what he told me."

I had the others lie down on the bed before I touched their wrists, transferring the data. When I was done, I had four sleeping guys in front of me. Mine. I didn't want to leave them while they were out cold, so I squeezed onto the top end of the bed and leaned against the wall. My head was pounding slightly, but the pain had gone. I really hoped it wouldn't hurt this much when Tim tried to talk to me on the planet. I couldn't fall unconscious every time he contacted me.

I looked at the guys. Even though he wasn't sleeping, Peter was snoring softly. I smiled. I was going to miss that sound, even though it kept me up at night. If Tim was right, I'd be on my own again soon. I had to savor every moment I had with these guys. Who knew how long it would take for us all to find each other again.

I ran my fingers along Kenny's biceps. His skin was soft and hard at the same time, but he had no scars on that side, unlike his other arm which was covered in them. Scars might be good to have on the slave planet, though. They showed that we weren't new to having to fight to survive. Even if I was going to have bleached hair, I wasn't going to look like a damsel in distress. Maybe that was the point of that. Women looking like dumb blonde bimbos. Not me.

Blake groaned, and I sat up straight, watching him intently. He didn't wake up, though. Hopefully, he wasn't in pain. I was surprised that Tim had offered to look for Blake first. That had to have been the nice Tim, the caring one. Once I actually met them, I'd have to find out if they had separate names. Tim One and Tim Two was a little cumbersome.

Sitting and watching them was making me tired. And I

needed to pee. I dozed for a bit, not wanting to leave them on their own. For a while, I tried to figure out what new knowledge Tim had supplied me with, but my mind felt like it always did, albeit a little sleepier. I assumed it would come to the surface when I needed it, just like it always happened with the alien tech.

I waited until Peter sleepily opened his eyes before leaving the room and heading to the bathroom. It was time to finally deal with my hair.

⸻◈⸻

I STARED at myself in the mirror. It looked wrong. Ugly. My hair was more orange than blonde, with uneven yellow streaks all over. I'd probably have to do it again to get rid of those reddish tones. Or maybe the alien bleach simply didn't work on human hair. Either way, I was pretty sure this wasn't going to be acceptable on the slave planet.

With a sigh, I turned away from the mirror. There was no point in doing it again right now, I'd only damage my hair further. Luckily, we still had some more time until we arrived at our destination.

The guys were in the living area, plates on their laps.

"We made you food," Kenny said with a grin as soon as I entered. "And what the fuck happened to you? Did you have an encounter with an angry bottle of orange juice?"

I rolled my eyes at him. "Thanks."

Blake handed me some toast, and I ate it. Still, Kenny continued to stare at me. I shook my head. "Okay, I get it. The hair is horrible. Awful. It turned out really badly. It's not like it was my idea to do this in the first place. I'm not looking for a change in my look or something."

Kenny sighed. "Come on. I'm going to dye your hair for you."

I gaped at him. "Pardon?"

"I'm going to dye your hair. Bleach it. Come on. At the end you won't look like this."

I put my hands on my hips. This was getting more insane by the day. "Kenny, why on Earth or space or whatever would you think it would turn out better for you?"

He took my hand. "Because I used to bleach my hair."

"You did?" It was hard for me to picture him doing that. Why would he bother?

"Yes, a million years ago, I used to do it to piss off my uncle. Long story. I used to do that purposefully so that he'd beat me and not my sister. Maybe. Or maybe not. Okay. Come on. It'll look pretty."

I let him lead me away back to the bathroom. His constant confusion of his background always broke my heart. He'd let his uncle *beat* him instead of his sister.

⟡

I STARED AT MY FINALLY-DONE-CORRECTLY, white-blonde hair. It was funny. I looked completely different, like a whole new person. I wondered if that was the point. We'd be new there, ready to be abused in whatever way they wanted to.

Kenny stared at me from behind me in the mirror. He'd had his hands on my hair for the last hour. It was sort of... hot.

He bent over to kiss my shoulder. "There now, that's better. Although, I miss your natural look."

"Thank you."

I didn't know what prompted me to do it, but I turned

around to face him. Without giving it any more thought than I just wanted to, I stroked my hand over the outside of his pants, cupping his cock.

He sucked in his breath. "Is this a thank you?"

I rolled my eyes but didn't let go of him. "Don't ruin it by saying something stupid."

I slipped my hands into his pants before I dropped the pants to the floor. His cock was hard, erect, and right there in front of me. I stroked him from tip to balls.

He closed his eyes. "You... undo me. You know that, right?"

I shook my head and gripped him harder. "No one undoes you, Kenny."

He opened his lids and met my gaze. In a heartbeat, he flipped me around so that I faced the mirror. He pulled down my pants. His eyes were on me in the mirror, and that was how I met his gaze.

"When I touch you, will you be wet?" he whispered in my ear.

"Touch me and find out." Everything with Kenny was a challenge. I loved that, but even as I pushed against his hand while he stroked me, I wondered if he ever wanted a break.

I leaned back on his chest, putting my head on his shoulder. "I trust you, you know."

His gaze flared. "What?"

"I trust you with my life, with my body, with me. I *trust* you."

He pushed himself inside of me. I hadn't known he was going to do that, hadn't realized he was about to. And that was okay. I loved the surprise. I moaned, and he bit down on my neck. It was going to leave a mark.

"I wasn't going to leave you. The second I saw you in that cage. You were mine to take care of, mine to worship."

I sighed. "Harder, Kenny. You can't hurt me. Harder."

He listened to me and pushed at me in a rougher jerk. It was what I wanted. His hand came around, gripping my neck. It was a gentle hold, not too tight, and I loved the slight bite of danger that always came with Kenny.

I rubbed one hand against my clit, helping me get further into the frenzy that was gripping both of us. I was wet, but I wasn't quite ready to come yet. Kenny groaned, his chest rumbling against my back while his teeth grazed my neck. He thrust in deep, leaving me breathless. This was what I'd been looking forward to. Raw, fast, untamed. It was the only way I could imagine being with Kenny for the first time.

His teeth held me in place while his hand slipped around until his fingers reached my breast. His nails bit into my skin, and I moaned again, the pain becoming one with pleasure. His thrusts grew harder, more desperate, while I flicked my clit, propelling myself to the edge.

"You're mine." He groaned, squeezing my breast.

"I'm yours," I whispered.

It didn't take much more than that to make us fall apart. Together we came, at the same time, our bodies pressed together, his thrusts becoming my undoing. I screamed as I let go, knowing that this was only the first of many times he would make me come. We were made for each other.

[21]

Time passes quickly when you don't want it to. As much as I tried to enjoy the time I was getting to spend with the guys, I could never quite forget that it was soon going to end. I wished I could have switched off that nagging voice in my head, but it seemed impossible for me to just live in the moment. I tried to distract myself as much as I could, but as soon as I had a moment to myself, those dark thoughts crept into my mind. How it might be the last time I ever slept with Blake. How I might never see Kenny's dimples again. How I might be sold to aliens and transported to the other end of the universe, far away from the men I loved.

"Penny for your thoughts?" Peter looked at me expectantly.

"What kind of currency do you think they have?" I asked randomly, not wanting to share my depressing musings. "Do the aliens have coins? Virtual money? Or are we their currency? One human is worth three dozen Klingons."

He laughed. "If that's the case, then you're the most valuable person in the entire universe."

"Did you just make a joke?"

"A compliment," he corrected. "Take it. It's yours. Now would you please step aside so I can get a hot drink?"

I realized I was still standing in front of one of the food machines. I'd been aimlessly staring at the selection on offer, wondering how the food would be on the slave planet.

"Sorry," I muttered, and let him take my place. "Can you—"

Pain shot through my skull, and I grabbed the edge of the counter to steady myself. I knew this pain by now. Tim was trying to contact me.

"Eileen?"

"Stop that pain," I groaned, very tempted to punch Tim. If he'd been in the room. I squeezed my eyes shut, knowing that it made it slightly more bearable.

"Sorry, my dear. It's urgent. There's been a change of plans. The auction is going to be held earlier than expected, so I've adjusted your ship's course. You'll arrive in about thirty-one Earth hours."

Panic rose up in me. "Wait, what? We're still supposed to have a week."

"What's going on?" Peter asked, his voice coming from far away. The pain was getting worse the longer Tim was connected to me.

"Thirty-one hours," Tim repeated. "I'm sorry, but there's no other way. If you miss the auction, you're going to be assigned to hard labor. You wouldn't survive that long enough until I can get you out. Get ready, and make sure your hair is bleached. You need to be presentable."

The pain disappeared and with it, Tim, leaving me speechless. Fuck.

"Thirty-one hours. Our auctions will be then so that we can avoid hard labor."

They'd been all happily chatting when I'd come in, and now silence struck us like a weapon exploding in the room.

Clay strode to the window, looking out. "Is no one going to bring up the possibility we never talk about?"

I wasn't sure I knew what he meant.

"We can opt out of this. When we went through the gates, we opted into this existence. No one explained what it was other than a chance to try to make a better life. It was a lie. We were thrown into this arena so that they could experiment on us with their new weapons. Day in and day out was hell."

Peter nodded. "True. But I'm not sure I'm following what you're saying here."

"We've made weapons on this ship. I don't know how we can use them once we get off the ship, but we have them. We can say no."

Blake shook his head. "I don't think we can do that. We opt out of being on this slave planet?"

"We blow ourselves and this ship up. We say no. We're not doing it."

My mind went blank for a second while I digested what he said to me. "Is that something that you want?"

"I'm not saying that. I'm simply stating that it is an option, and before we start plotting anything else, I think we should acknowledge it as a possibility. Put it on the table. There is a big giant opt out."

He was right. It was unpleasant to think about, but there it was. "That's an all or nothing thing. We'd all have to want that."

"If individually we did," Kenny spoke in a low voice. "But not as a whole, the poison is an option."

I groaned. This was awful. Our vacation on this ship

was really over. Back to real life. "Does anyone want that? Speak truthfully."

I had to force myself to look at Blake. But I didn't see resignation on his face, not then anyway.

"I don't want to die." Peter spoke first. "It might be dumb, but I feel hopeful. We survived that existence. I might eat my words later, but right now, I think the five of us can do anything."

There were really seven of us. The two Tims were along for this ride, strange as it was. I didn't bring that up right now. They weren't attached to Tim the way I was.

Blake took my hand. "You might be surprised to hear this, but I'm also... not interested in the out. I want to believe that this is something we can get through."

"Me neither," Kenny said simply. "I'm going out in a blaze of glory. That's what I want."

I'd deal with that statement later. "Clay?"

He turned to look at me. "Eileen? You know what could happen to women. I mean, why did you have to dye your hair? Is that sexually appealing to these aliens? Things can go badly for men, too, but we all know what happens to women more often than not. We won't even be with you. What do you want?"

I walked to him. "Not this option. Not yet, anyway." I had to hear his answer. "What do you want?"

"I want a future. With all of you. Somehow, I want to keep this. We're like the most dysfunctional family ever, but it's ours. I'm not going anywhere."

Kenny grinned, reminding me of his crazy old self. "That's settled then. No blowing ourselves up. We're going to get through this. We survived Purgatory, and now we're going to survive Hell."

Peter began to clap, slowly, dramatically. "Well said.

Such a rousing speech. Now what shall we do for the time we have left? As much as I'd like to think we've made enough weapons, we could probably make some more. Who knows what awaits us there."

Blake groaned. "I'd much rather just spend time with Eileen."

"Thirty-one hours, that's almost eight hours for each of us with her," Kenny said, still grinning.

I glared at him. "I'm not a slave yet who gets assigned work hours. And yes, I want to spend time with you all, but let's do it together. We can build weapons, prepare ourselves, snuggle. All of us, together."

Kenny shrugged. "Okay, then. When you say snuggle, together, does that mean..."

Suddenly, all the guys' eyes were on me. My cheeks flushed. "No. I don't think I'm ready for that. I meant snuggling, like all of us in the same bed, touching—"

"Fucking," Clay interrupted. "Please?"

Did these men ever think of anything else? Now that I'd slept with all of them, it was hard to stop thinking of how they'd felt. Their bodies pressed against mine. Being connected in that most magical way. But no, I wasn't going to spend the last thirty-one hours in bed. I was going to prepare to fight for their lives and my own. Sex could come after. Our reward when we were all reunited again. Something to look forward to.

I shook my head. "No, let's get to work."

In a way, I hated this rational side of me, but I'd learned that in order to survive, you sometimes had to ignore your desires and focus on what was most important. In this case, being as prepared as possible.

"I think we should decide on what to wear when we arrive," I announced. They looked at me blankly.

"Are you planning to put on a fashion show?" Clay asked with a frown. "Not sure that's going to work."

"No, but our current clothes aren't very practical. Not enough pockets to carry supplies, and no way to hide weapons. I doubt the aliens who stocked this ship thought of any of that." I grimaced. "And I'd really like some underwear if I'm to be sold as a slave."

Kenny raised his hand. "I know how to sew. I've not seen any needles around, but I'm sure I could fashion one from all the junk metal we have lying around."

I didn't ask how he knew how to do that. Probably something to do with his sister that he might or might not have had. One day, I'd ask him to tell me his story—his real one If he could remember it. But not now. We couldn't afford to linger on the past. It wouldn't help us survive the future. Let him not remember. It had to be a survival thing for him.

"Good. Let's collect all the clothes we have and make ourselves some proper warrior outfits."

We got busy doing that. I took all of the clothes in the closets and brought them to Kenny. He and Clay were tearing them apart. In the other room, the brothers were opening and closing drawers. All of these weeks, and we still didn't know everything that was on this ship.

I sat down. "What can I do?"

Kenny winked at me. "Tear away, baby."

The truth was we were good at this. Working together. Doing things. We'd been sent out to survive or die, to kill each other trying. But here we were, a unit that worked. Even if we were all a little bit fucked up.

When Peter came in and handed Clay scissors, I smiled at him. Leave it to Peter to find what we needed. A thought dawned on me. "How are we going to handle it when we land? Are we going to just be easy? Go out fighting? What are we going to do with our weapons?"

Blake sighed, lying down with his head in my lap. I smiled. He did that a lot. Apparently, he wasn't going to be participating in the sewing. Peter rolled his eyes, but there was no malice there. This was our routine.

From my lap, Blake answered. "We don't have any idea what to expect. Presumably, they transport people to this planet to do this all the time. I imagine they sort of know how to handle us."

That was a daunting thought. Handle us in what way?

Was this some kind of routine? We needed answers, and we needed them now. I hated not being able to plan. I didn't want to wake up in another cage with no idea what to do again. If Kenny hadn't been there, I'd have been screwed.

"I love this." I just had to say it. "I love us. I love all of you."

I gripped the sides of my chair, staring at the planet racing toward us. Actually, it was us doing the racing, but it didn't look that way. I really hoped the spaceship knew what it was doing. Alarms had started ringing an hour ago, followed by an automatic message telling us to get strapped in. Now we were on the bridge, hurtling through space, with our destination getting ever bigger on the screen before us.

The planet didn't look at all like Earth from space. There was barely any blue or green, just dark red and ochre hues, with a few streaks of purple. I guess I shouldn't have expected an alien world to look the same as our own home planet. Did they have water? Were those purple things oceans? Would there even be breathable air?

"Is it supposed to be this bumpy?" Blake shouted over the noise.

The spaceship was shaking, and the sound of groaning metal made my insides clench in fear. Until an hour ago, we'd barely noticed the ship's engines, but now they were roaring and humming as they propelled us toward the planet.

I forced myself to look at the guys in the seats next to me. Clay seemed awestruck, his gaze fixed on the screen, his eyes wide. Peter was the opposite. He had his eyes pinched shut and was gripping the chair's armrests so tight, his knuckles were bright white. Kenny was laughing. I shouldn't have been surprised about that. He still had a bit of his old crazy left. For him, this seemed nothing more than a rollercoaster ride. Me, I was tense, but at the same time, I couldn't help but be a little excited. We were about to set foot on another planet. Never, ever would I have imagined doing that. We might be the first humans ever to land here.

The forces pressing me into the chair increased. Breathing was getting harder.

"Loss of consciousness imminent," the robotic voice announced just as black fog began to roll over my vision. Thanks for the warning.

"Hold on," I tried to say, but my tongue was heavy, and darkness took me.

⬥

A LOUD BANGING sound woke me, and I sat up straight, looking around me in alarm. The ship was no longer moving, nor could I hear the engines. We'd landed.

I opened my seat belt and got to my feet. My head hurt, but not much. The guys were still unconscious, slumped in their seats, held up by their belts. Blake was closest to me. I shook him by the shoulder, and he groaned, slowly opening his eyes.

"How's the weather out there?" he asked.

I chuckled. "No idea, the screen is off. But the banging makes me think that someone wants us to come outside."

"Are we there yet?" Kenny sat up, blinking at me with a goofy smile. "Is that the locals trying to establish contact?"

The banging got more intense. We better get ready before they forced their way into the ship. I doubted that would endear us with our future slave masters.

"Peter? Clay?" I went over to them and gave them each a gentle shake. It took Clay the longest to wake up. By the time he was finally coherent, the rest of us had already changed into our new clothes. We'd decided to leave the big weapons on the ship, hidden all over the place, and only take whatever we could conceal with us. We didn't want them to see us as a threat and attack us on sight. Whoever they were going to be.

More banging.

"Guys, let's hurry up," I said, running a hand through my bleached hair. I hated the color, but if it would keep me safe, so be it.

Without talking about it, we linked our hands and slowly walked to the loading dock. This was our last moment alone.

"I love you," I whispered, my voice choking up. "Stay safe."

Before the others could reply, the air lock opened without warning, revealing a snapshot of the world outside. A figure stepped into view, his features hidden in shadows. He had four arms. Oh my fucking goodness. An alien with four arms. I'd seen it many times, but it never ceased to amaze me. Like I was constantly having to believe it again. He said something in a guttural language, but I didn't need a translator to understand that he wanted us to follow him.

"We can do this." Blake squeezed my hand. "We'll make it."

I took a deep breath and let go of their hands. I didn't want the aliens to think us weak. They might exploit our relationship if they found out about it. Clenching my fists, I followed the alien outside, walking down a ramp that they'd pushed against our ship.

Hot air blasted into my face, and I blinked, trying to get the sand out of my eyes. The shouts of hundreds of people reached my ears. Were they on our side or waiting to watch us die?

I stood up straight, glaring at the aliens in front of me. My men were at my side. Tim, the two Tims, were out there somewhere. They'd find us and get us out of here.

We'd survived Purgatory. Now we were going to survive Hell.

THE END

Don't fret, dear reader.
We are hard at work on book two....

For now, subscribe to our newsletters to be kept up to date
with this series and other books:
rebeccaroyce.com
skyemackinnon.com/newsletter

As a teenager, I would hide in my room to read my favorite romance novels when I was supposed to be doing my homework.

I am the mother of three adorable boys and I am fortunate to be married to my best friend. I live in Austin Texas where I am determined to eat all the barbecue in town.

I am in love with science fiction, fantasy, and the paranormal and try to use all of these elements in my writing. I've been told I'm a little bloodthirsty so I hope that when you read my work you'll enjoy the action packed ride that always ends in romance. I love to write series because I love to see characters develop over time and it always makes me happy to see my favorite characters make guest appearances in other books.

In my world anything is possible, anything can happen, and you should suspect that it will.

I'd love to hear from you! Please visit my website at www. rebeccaroyce.com to sign up for my newsletter and learn about my books!

Here's where you can find me online:

- Rebecca's Randomness Reading Group https:// www.facebook.com/ groups/RebeccasRandomness/

- https://www.rebeccaroyce.com
- MeWe: RebeccaRoyce

www.ingramcontent.com/pod-product-compliance
Lightning Source LLC
Chambersburg PA
CBHW050852190726
48286CB00007B/2342